From Here to There

A Collection of Short Stories

From Here to There

A Collection of Short Stories

By

Rodney Riesel

Published by Island Holiday Publishing

East Greenbush, NY

ISBN: 978-0-9971149-1-1

First Edition

Special thanks to:

Pamela Guerriere

Kevin Cook

Cover Design by:

Connie Fitsik

To obtain more copies of this book friend me at

https://www.facebook.com/rodneyriesel

For Brenda

Kayleigh, Ethan,

&

Peyton

Contents

Carl and Sandy

"Salvatore's, how can I help you?"

"I would like to order a large pizza," Carl said.

"What would you like on that?" asked the girl at the other end.

"Pepperoni, mushrooms, and sausage."

"Name?"

"Reed."

"Okay, give us about … thirty minutes."

"I would like that delivered."

"Can I have your address?"

"704, Walnut Street."

"Okay, give us about forty-five minutes."

"Yup. Thanks." Carl hung up the phone, stood motionless for a second and then walked through the kitchen, down the hall, and up the stairs. At the end of the upstairs hallway was the master bedroom. Carl entered and stared at the huge pile of clothing on the bed. *Where to start?* He thought.

Carl picked up one of the sweaters and held it by the shoulders. He folded one sleeve, then the other, and doubled it over into a neat little square. He glanced back at the cardboard box that sat on the floor next to him and then reached back with his foot and slid it closer to the bed. He dropped the sweater into the box and picked up another.

"What are you doing?" Sandy asked, as she entered the bedroom.

Carl jumped. "Jesus Christ! Don't do that. Why do you have to sneak up on me like that?"

Sandy snickered. "Sorry. I thought you heard me."

"Well I didn't."

Sandy walked over and sat at the foot of the bed. "So what are you doing?"

"Folding up these old clothes." He dropped another sweater into the box and picked up a pair of jeans.

"Old? I bought those like three months ago."

"Do you wear them?" Carl asked.

"No," Sandy answered.

"Okay then," he said, laying the jeans in the box, on top of the sweaters. "Out they go."

Sandy shook her head. She watched Carl fold and pack for a few more minutes and then stood up to turn on the television. She sat back down. "Can you hand me the remote?"

Carl reached over, grabbed the remote control that was lying on the night stand and tossed it to Sandy. She flipped through the stations until she came to an old episode of King of Queens and stopped. She tossed the remote on the bed behind her.

Carl shot her a look, picked up the remote and laid it back on the night stand.

"I loved this show," Sandy said.

"Me too." Carl didn't look up, he just kept to his task.

Sandy stared at the TV. "How long has this show been off the air now?"

"I don't know, six or seven years, maybe."

"Huh, doesn't seem that long."

"Time flies when you're having fun," Carl responded, in a sarcastic tone.

"Hey," Sandy scolded, "We had fun."

"Some of us had more fun than others."

"Stop. There's no reason for that."

"I know."

"What did you do?"

"Does it matter?" Carl asked.

Sandy turned back toward the television.

When the box was full Carl closed the flaps, locking each flap under the one next to it. Then he bent down and pushed the box across the carpeting up against the dresser. He took hold of another box and sat it next to the closet door.

"What's next?" Sandy asked.

"Pocket books or boots, I guess," Carl answered, as he pulled open the closet door. "Holy shit, you sure jammed a lot of crap in here."

"Crap? There's nothing in there that's crap."

Carl reached up on the shelf and grabbed one of the purses. When he yanked it out, three other purses toppled down on top of him. He showed the purse to his wife.

"That's certainly not crap. I love that purse."

"I can tell, by exactly how many times I've seen you actually use it."

"I used it all the time."

Carl dropped it into the empty box. "Name one time."

"The day I bought it. Remember? We had lunch at that little place in Cooperstown, the place where you walk down the stairs. After we ordered I took everything out of the purse I was carrying and put it in that one."

"I remember … I remember everything."

"You had that steak and greens panini and I had the Greek wrap."

"I remember."

"I wonder why we never went back there."

Carl dropped two more pocket books into the box. "We never went back there because a few months later I found out you ate dinner there with what's-his-name."

Sandy turned her head back toward the television. "I guess you do remember everything, and you never fail to bring it up. I said I was sorry."

"And that made it all better."

"What more could I have done?"

"You could have tried not being sorry for a second and third time."

Sandy got up from the bed and walked over to the box. She leaned over and picked up the first purse he had dropped in. "I want to keep this one." She turned and before she could get away Carl snatched the purse from her hand and threw it back in the box.

"You're not keeping anything," he said. "You can't keep anything."

Sandy sat back down on the bed. "We all make mistakes."

"Most of us don't make so many of them."

"Oh no? Why don't you tell me what *you* did?"

"Because it doesn't matter."

"So nothing *you* did matters."

Carl just shook his head. When the second box was full he closed it and stacked it on top of the first box. As he went to retrieve another box, he stumbled over one of Sandy's shoes. He almost fell, but caught himself on the dresser.

Sandy chuckled. "Clumsy, much?" she joked.

Carl looked back at her and smiled, but quickly wiped it away.

"Do you love me?" Sandy asked.

"Does it matter?"

"It matters to me."

"When did that start?" Carl almost tripped over the shoe again, this time he kicked it across the room.

Sandy chuckled again. "Remember that time we were in Maine and you twisted you ankle on that boulder?"

"I remember … I remember everything."

"Oh yeah, I forgot. That was fun."

"What was fun?"

"The trip to Maine, silly."

"*I* thought it was fun." Carl said.

"Why do you say it like that?"

"Because it wasn't real, Sandy. Don't you get it? It was only that one moment in time. It was only fun for that fraction of a second that we were *having* fun. Everything wasn't fun. I tripped over a fucking boulder and we laughed, that was it. It's like when someone smiles for a photograph, they're not always smiling; it's just for that micro-second it takes for the shutter to open and close. Fuck!"

"Sorry," Sandy said softly, her voice shaky. "I had fun. I had a *lot* of fun … with you."

Carl stood motionless staring into the empty box. "If that's true, then why are we here, like this, now?"

"Because of you. What did you do?"

"It doesn't matter!" Carl grabbed a pair of brown leather boots off the closet floor and shot them in the box. Sandy remained quiet as she watched her favorite boots go inside, one by one.

The credits rolled and the theme song played and another episode began. Sandy laid back and rested her head on a few tops and sweaters that were still lying on the bed. The characters traded jabs and recited funny lines but Sandy was in no mood to laugh. A tear escaped her eye and ran down over her ear and dripped on the bed. She tried to think of something she could say that might make Carl smile, or maybe even laugh out loud. It broke her heart remembering how much Carl used to laugh.

"Remember when you bought these in Florida?" Carl asked.

Sandy turned her head to see the pair of black leather boots Carl held in his hand. They had a four-inch wedged heel and Sandy remembered that they came up past her knee. "You said I looked like Gene Simmons from Kiss."

"You did. I waited for you to burst into Detroit Rock City at any moment."

"Where did I get *those boots*?"

"Atlantic City."

"Oh yeah, it was so hot that summer. I remember walking along the board walk sweating my ass off."

"Uh-huh."

"Remember that sea food restaurant? That was so good."

"I remember."

"It took so long for the food to come, I had four margaritas and you practically had to carry me back to the room."

Carl finished with the boots and there was still some room for some more pocket books so he filled the box the rest of the way with the few that remained and then shut the closet door.

"I'm getting hungry," Sandy said.

"Me too."

"You want to order a pizza or something?"

"I already did," Carl explained and checked his watch.

"What did you order?"

"Large pizza."

"What did you get on it?"

"Mushrooms, sausage, and pepperoni."

"You know I don't like pepperoni."

Carl slid the last box over next to the other two. "I know, but what does that matter now?" he walked over and sat on the edge of the bed. Sandy reached back and put her hand on his shoulder. He pulled away. "Don't, your hands are cold."

"Sorry," said Sandy and placed the palm of her hand against her own cheek. "They're not *that* cold." She cupped her hands together and blew into them to warm them up. She then placed her hand on the back of his neck and massaged it with her finger tips.

Carl shifted his shoulders. "Didn't help," he said.

"Sorry. I don't know what you expect me to do about it."

"I don't expect you to do anything."

The doorbell rang and Carl jumped up from the bed.

"Pizza's here," Sandy exclaimed.

Carl left the bedroom and walked down the hallway. When he got to the top of the stairs he bent down so he could see out through the glass panel in the front door. When he saw it was the delivery girl he went quickly down the stairs and answered the door.

"How are you this evening, Mr. Reed?"

"Good … I guess," Carl answered.

The girl gave Carl a look of sadness and cocked her head to the side. "Sorry about … you know," she whispered.

Carl took the pizza from the young girl. "I know," he answered, and then searched the back of his mind for the delivery girl's name.

"Lori," she reminded him.

"Yes, Lori." Carl sat the pizza box on the wooden bench that sat in the hall under the window and then reached into his pocket for his money clip. He pulled out a twenty and a ten and handed it to Lori. "Here ya go, you can keep the change."

"Thanks Mr. Reed," Lori said, she spun on her heels, walked back across the porch and down the steps toward her car. Carl watched to make sure she was safe inside her vehicle before shutting the front door and flipping off the porch light.

When Carl got back to the kitchen he sat the pizza box on the counter, grabbed a plate out of the cupboard, and sat it on the counter top next to the pizza. He went to the refrigerator, opened the door, and studied its contents. On the second shelf from the top was a half-full, twelve ounce, bottle of Diet Pepsi. Carl stared at it for a second and then picked it up and took it over to the trash can and threw it away. He returned to the fridge and grabbed a can of ginger ale. He put ice in a glass, opened the soda can, and poured it into the glass. He then put two pieces of pizza on his plate, picked up his glass and went into the living room.

With a slice of pizza in one hand and the remote control in the other, Carl scanned the program guide for something to watch.

"How's your pizza?" Sandy asked.

"Good," Carl answered.

"I'd have a piece, if you hadn't gotten pepperoni on it."

Carl glanced over at her and lowered one eyebrow. "That's why?"

"That's part of the reason." Sandy walked in and sat down on the love seat that was against the opposite wall from the couch. "What are you watching?"

"I haven't decided yet." Carl searched for a program until he came to an old episode of Star Trek and then hit select on the remote.

"Ugh!" Sandy said.

Carl ignored her.

"I this is what you're watching?"

"Yup."

"I hate this show."

"Don't watch."

Sandy stared at the screen anyway as Kirk and Spock discussed a plan to eliminate this episodes alien threat. "Remember when we were first dating and we stayed up all night that time watching those old movies, the one with the giant chicken?"

"I remember," Carl answered, never taking his eyes from the screen.

"We used to lay on the couch together back then."

"Uh-huh … and then we didn't anymore."

"I wonder why we stopped doing that."

"Probably for the same reason we stopped showering together, stopped running together, stopped sleeping naked, stopped holding hands, stopped trying to have children, stopped saying I love you. Should I go on?" Carl took another bite of his pizza and then a swig of his soda.

"What was the name of that movie?" Sandy asked.

"What movie?"

"The one with the giant chicken."

"*Mysterious Island.*"

"Boy, you do remember everything. I liked that movie."

"Me too."

"I wish it was on now, and we could lie together on the couch and watch it."

"I wish a lot of things, but it's too late for that now."

Sandy watched her husband as he finished up his second piece of pizza. "Do you still want me to leave?" she asked.

"I never wanted you to leave," he answered. "That's why I never asked you to leave. That's why I always tried to work it out; time after time. Over and over again."

"I said I was sorry."

"I know. You said you were sorry every time you got caught. You were only sorry *when* you got caught."

"You think I'm a horrible person."

"I don't think you're anything. None of it matters now. It's not like we're just going to wipe the slate clean of everything that's happened."

"We could have."

"Maybe … but probably not. It's too late now, anyway, so let's stop talking about it. Christ, maybe if we had of talked this much before, we *could* have worked it out."

"I'm just not one to talk about things."

"And yet you can't stop talking."

"Whoa, wouldn't want to interrupt an important episode of Star Track."

"It's Star *Trek*. Maybe if you had paid more attention to me and less attention to others, you would know that."

"Full of criticism right till the end."

"Yeah that's me," Carl said as he stood and made his way back into the kitchen. "Always criticizing your infidelity. How dare me."

When Carl returned to the living room he had another slice of pizza on his plate and had refilled his drink.

"You want me to put the rest of that pizza on a plate and put it in the fridge?" Sandy asked.

"That would be great," Carl answered.

Sandy got up from the love seat and left the room.

Carl could hear the cabinet door open and the plate being removed. He could hear the plastic wrap as it was ripped from its container. He knew he was going to miss the sounds of someone else in the house. He wondered if he had made a mistake.

When Sandy opened the refrigerator door she called out, "you never ate the rest of this macaroni and cheese I made."

"Well, it's over a week old, so I'm not going to eat it now," Carl hollered back.

"You want me to throw it out?"

"If you want."

Sandy placed the plate of pizza on the top shelf and then removed the bowl of macaroni and cheese. "Don't let the rest of this pizza go to waste."

"Yup."

Sandy closed the door and carried the bowl to the trash can. She pressed the pedal raising the lid, and with a wooden spoon she scraped the mac and cheese into the garbage. She filled the sink with water, washed the few dishes that were in there, dried them, and put them away. She took one last look around the kitchen and went back into the living room. "I did the dishes," she informed Carl.

"Thanks," he replied.

"I have to go now."

A chill ran up Carl's spine, as though the room's temperature had dropped several degrees. "I know."

"I love you."

"I loved you too."

"No matter what you think, I always did love you, and I will love you forever."

Sandy's words gave Carl little comfort. He reached up and with his index finger wiped away a tear.

"Will you miss me?" Sandy asked.

"I already do."

"Are you going to tell me what you did?"

"I can't."

Sandy glanced down at Carl's half eaten slice of pizza. "Did you put something in my food?"

"No."

"Then what?"

"It was the protein drink," Carl said quietly. "Every day before you went to the gym."

Sandy smiled. "You put something in my drink. Not too healthy after all."

Carl shrugged his shoulders. "Sorry."

Sandy turned and Carl watched as she faded off into nothing.

Impaled

An Adirondack Short Story

ONE

Leah rubbed her hands together and jumped up and down, trying to keep herself warm. "We should have waited until tomorrow morning," she said, blowing warm air into her cupped hands.

"But then it wouldn't have been our wedding night," Colin replied. He knelt over the instructions to the four-man tent he had purchased three days earlier, his only light coming from the headlights of Leah's black 2011 Volkswagen Passat.

"You should have put it together once in the backyard before trying it in total darkness," Leah commented.

Despite his bride's mounting impatience, Colin kept to the task at hand. "Is there anything else I should have done?"

Leah scanned the darkness for beasts she had only seen in her dreams. "I hope there's nothing out there that will eat us."

"It's the Adirondacks, not the Serengeti."

Leah's head snapped to her right, and her eyes pierced the darkness. "I thought I heard something."

"I keep hearing something too," Colin replied sarcastically. He looked up at a shivering Leah. "Why don't you get in the car if you're cold?"

Leah complied without hesitation. As she had stated from the onset of Colin's honeymoon plans, *camping was not her thing.* But she went along with it because he had obliged her wedding plans without complaint.

Leah pulled a thin blanket from the pile of camping supplies in the backseat and wrapped it around her shoulders. She looked over at the empty tent box that lay in the passenger seat. *Ten minute setup time*, she read and grinned. From where she now sat and watched, it was beginning to look like camping wasn't Colin's thing either. He admitted that he hadn't been camping in years, not since he was a kid, but it was something that he wanted to start doing again now that he was a husband and hopefully soon a father. He had confessed to Leah that some of his happiest times as a child were while camping with his family.

Colin was twenty-seven years old, six feet tall, with brown hair that was thinning much sooner than he had hoped. He had a slender build with long legs and gangly arms that matched his big hands with long thin fingers and large feet. It had been almost three years since that Thursday night in Utica when Leah had first met him, and her friends joked that if the rest of Colin's body was in proportion to his feet and hands, she was in for a fun night. It would be three weeks later at his small apartment on Genesee Street that she would finally have that fun night discovering that everything *was* in proportion.

Leah pulled her cell phone from her back pocket and browsed through the photos she had taken at the reception earlier in the evening. She smiled as her finger slid across the screen, flipping from one photo to the other. She had only been a wife for about six hours, but it was something she could remember looking forward to for most of her life. As an inner excitement warmed her, she ran her hands through her blond, curly shoulder-length hair.

Petite at slightly under five feet, Leah's stature was a contrast to her new husband's. But it was her beautiful smile that first caught Colin's attention with her perfectly straight, white teeth. She had small breasts that barely filled her A cup bra, but that was not a problem for Colin. He was an ass man, and hers was perfect.

Colin opened the back door, startling Leah. "I pitched the tent," he said proudly.

"I hope so; it is our wedding night after all," Leah joked.

Colin grabbed the blankets, pillows, and sleeping bags from the backseat. "Ha, good one," he said with a chuckle. "Now get in that tent and get naked."

"Finally," Leah remarked, climbing out of the front seat.

Collin zipped open the front of the tent and threw the blankets inside. Leah ambled in and began making the sleeping bags and blankets into a comfortable bed.

As Leah set to creating their evening's love nest, Colin's stomach rumbled. The reception food was making its way toward the exit. "I'm gonna run up to the bathroom."

"Hurry up, baby," Leah said. "I'll be naked and all alone in these dark woods; no telling what might happen to me."

Colin turned toward the trail that led to the restrooms. "I'll be back as quick as I can. Feel free to start without me."

"I just might do that," Leah called out to his retreating back.

Leah continued to spread the blankets out on the nylon floor of the tent. It was way too quiet and dark; she hoped Colin would be back soon.

Deeper in the forest, Colin made his way up the dark trail, sticks snapping under his feet. Through the trees he could see the yellow light shining through the restroom windows. He knew where he was going, but he wished he brought a flashlight. The trail exited onto the blacktop road that winded through the woods to every campsite. He walked down the road past another camp and finally to the restrooms. The door creaked loudly as he opened it.

Leah sat on the blankets in the middle of the tent. She heard a branch snap and told herself there was nothing to be afraid of. With both hands, she grabbed the bottom hem of her shirt and pulled it over her head. She waited a few seconds and then unbuttoned her jeans, and then unzipped them. She lifted her rear and slid the jeans down to her feet and kicked them off, tossing them to the edge of the makeshift bed.

Back at the restroom, Colin sat on the toilet; it was his turn to look through the evening's pictures on *his* phone. He paused at the photo of his beautiful wife on the dance floor. He remembered how she looked, her dress sweeping the floor as she danced with her father.

Snap! Leah bolted upright. "Colin?" She sat alone in the dark tent, her eyes skimming from wall to wall. A shadow passed by the back of the tent. Leah closed her eyes tightly. *It's only your imagination, it's only your imagination*, she told herself as she searched the tent floor for the flashlight. As quietly as she could, she wiggled out from under the blankets, then crawled to her shirt. She slipped it back over her head and unzipped the tent flap. The sound of the zipper seemed deafening against the eerie silence of evening.

Leah slowly stuck her head out through the opening. She could see puffs of her own breath in the cold night air as her breathing grew more rapid and she could almost smell the wetness of the leaves, trees, and dirt.

Leaves crunched in the darkness and she clicked on the flashlight. "Colin? Colin, this isn't funny," she called into the darkness. There was no answer. She climbed out of the tent, stood, and pulled her t-shirt down over her butt cheeks. With her flashlight she lit up the forest, first shining it in one direction and then sweeping it in the other. When she was satisfied there was nothing there, she looked in the direction of the restrooms and decided to join her husband. She turned, bent over, and reached through the opening for her flip-flops. As she grabbed them both in one hand, she stood, turned, and felt the skin of her abdomen pop as cold, sharp steel entered the front of her body and exited through the back. The flip-flops and flashlight left her tiny hands and fell to the ground at her feet. For a second there was unbearable pain… and then none as she looked up into the eyes of a stranger.

"Why?" she whispered. Her throat rattled as she tried to inhale. She opened her mouth to scream, but the stranger placed a gloved hand over it, smothering any sound. She felt the warmth of her own urine as it ran down her legs and puddled at her feet, and then her last breath escaped through her nose and all went black.

Colin whistled as he made his way back down the pine needle-covered path toward his campsite. He thought of his wife's naked body as she lay beneath the sleeping bags awaiting his arrival. They had made love hundreds of times in the past, but this was different, for tonight he was her husband. As he came to the end of the path he could see the light of the flashlight lying in the dirt. "Leah," he called out as he bent to pick it up. When he rose, he shined the flashlight around the perimeter of the campsite pausing on a tree a few yards away. There he saw his bride wearing nothing but a t-shirt, her lifeless body staked to the tree. He started to take a stumbling step toward her when he felt a sharp pain on the back of his skull. The cold blackness of the late spring Adirondack night flashed white and he crumpled to the wet ground with a thud.

TWO

"Chuck, get up," his wife nagged. "That alarm's been buzzing for twenty minutes."

Chuck yawned as he turned over in bed and stretched his arms above his head, driving his knuckles into the headboard. He fought to open his eyes, squinting at the bright morning sunshine. *Why does she have to open the blinds first thing every morning?* he thought. Chuck heard each step creak as his wife, Alice, made her way back down the stairs of the old farm house and into the kitchen. Twenty-three years in the same house and it was easy to tell who was in which room just by the sounds of the old wooden floors.

Chuck swung his legs over the side of the bed and sat there for a second searching the room for his robe. *Holy shit, what's the temperature?* he wondered. It was the first week of June, but sitting there in nothing but his red and blue checkered flannel boxers, it felt more like the first week of April. Chucks hairy chest and beard were not quite enough to keep him warm this morning.

Chuck was a big man, two hundred and sixty pounds of hairy forest ranger. At six-foot-six he towered over everyone he knew. He wore thick black hair a little longer than regulations allowed and his beard, just as black, had undergone twelve years of cultivating. At his age he should have been showing a little gray, but there was none, which brought ribbings from his friends and co-workers about how often he dyed his hair. The big man had celebrated his fiftieth birthday the night before and was having a hard time shaking off the evening's fun.

Finding his red flannel robe on the back of the bathroom door and putting it on, he stood in front of the medicine cabinet mirror. He wondered what he now looked like under the beard. Did he look the same as he did when he started growing it? Does keeping a beard for that many years keep your face looking younger, or does it make you look even older when you shave it? All questions to be answered at a later date, he figured.

As he stepped off the bottom stair, Chuck peeked into the living room. Cartoons played on the television. Bobby, seven years old, lay in a chair, his head on one armrest and his legs hanging over the other. John, six years old, knelt on the floor with his elbows on the ottoman. Chuck Jr., five years old, lay on the couch wrapped in an old blue Snuggie.

"Good morning, boys," Chuck greeted them.

There was no answer, and no one's eyes left the television. Chuck looked up at the clock that hung on the wall over the kitchen sink. *Six o'clock*, he thought. *Can't get them out of bed on a school day, but they're up before six on the weekend.*

There was no aroma of bacon, eggs, potatoes, or toast this morning, and Chuck was a little disappointed. "Any breakfast?"

"Your birthday was yesterday," Alice joked. She was pouring the last drops of beer into the sink from the Old Milwaukee cans and rinsing each one. Shaking the water from each can she placed them in a plastic bag.

Chuck poured himself a cup of coffee. "Oh yeah." He took a seat at the kitchen table and slid the morning newspaper in front of himself.

"You want some toast?"

"Yeah, put a couple pieces in for me."

"Sure, I'm not doing anything," Alice replied with a hint of sarcasm.

Bobby pulled up a chair next to his father. "I'm hungry."

"There's cereal in the cupboard," his mother responded.

"Can you make it for me?"

"No."

"You're making Dad's toast."

"Get a job and buy some cereal and then I'll make your cereal every morning."

"I'm too young to get a job."

"Then go clean your room."

"I hate cleaning my room."

"I hate making cereal."

Alice buttered the toast and handed it to Chuck as he got up from the table. He took a bite. "I gotta jump in the shower and get to work," he said. "It's getting late."

THREE

Eric Stone pulled his black 2004 Ford F-150 into the parking lot of the Town of Webb Police Station. He didn't usually work Sundays, but he volunteered weeks ago to work this Sunday for someone else. It seemed like a good idea at the time, but crawling out of a warm bed on a cold foggy Sunday morning wasn't easy.

Stone had been an investigator for the Town of Webb Police Department for six years, and he loved his job. It was the rest of his life that he wasn't too happy about. Six years ago when he came home and told his wife that he had gotten the job in Webb, she was excited. She claimed she had always wanted to live in a place like Old Forge, so they packed up their stuff and moved from Binghamton to a small house on Big Moose Road in Eagle Bay. Two years later the complaints of boredom started. Stone told his wife, "You gotta get out and do things, meet people, get a hobby or something." So that winter Emily decided to take skiing lessons from a young man in Old Forge. Within a few weeks the skiing lessons turned into sex lessons and that spring she moved out. He heard she was living back in Binghamton, but after two years of no communication, he didn't know facts from rumors.

Stone removed his jacket and hung it on the old wooden coat rack that stood next to the door. Short for a cop at five-foot, eight, he wore his peppered hair short, military style. A few years ago he had a slight belly that hung over his belt, but since his wife left he had gotten in better shape, adding muscle to his stature and making it easier to pick up the occasional waitress, bartender, or tourist.

Rolling the chair out from under the big oak desk, Stone took a seat, grabbed the remote control off of the desk, and leaned back, propping up his feet. He turned on the television and flipped through the stations. *Not much to watch at seven o'clock on a Sunday morning*, he thought. Stone figured he would watch TV for a while and then make his rounds. A nice quiet day.

FOUR

Chuck Little pulled up in front of the ranger station at Nick's Lake in his white Dodge Ram. Mel was already sitting in the booth at the gate. Chuck waved and Mel gave him the thumbs-up.

The fog had started to thin, letting the sun shine through to begin its process of warming the Adirondack forest. Chuck looked up through the towering pines at the sun and felt it warm his cheeks. He could smell the campfires of the early risers. Sundays were usually quiet; weekenders would all be gone by eleven, and the ones staying for the week wouldn't be bored yet, so they would just hang around the campsite.

Mel watched as Chuck headed through the front door of the station and return moments later without his jacket. "Looks like it's gonna warm up pretty quick today," Mel said.

"It does," Chuck answered.

Mel pointed at a small piece of paper on the desk. "Someone left a note on the door before I got here this morning. It said they spotted a bear in the D loop."

"That's weird that someone spotted a bear out here in the woods," Chuck replied sarcastically.

Mel laughed. "Yeah, go figure."

"Did you take a ride through yet?"

"No, I got here a couple minutes before you."

Chuck grabbed a clip board that hung from a nail on the wall. "I'll go. See if anyone came in last night after dark."

Mel nodded and Chuck was on his way. The sign said, SLOW 10 MPH, and Chuck kept the speedometer right at ten as he made his way from loop to loop.

Chuck stopped his truck in loop C and looked at the black Volkswagen Passat parked in campsite number fifty-one. *Must have arrived after dark*, he thought. Picking up his clipboard off of the seat he wrote down the license plate number, then pulled his truck to the side of the road and parked. Clipboard in hand he walked by the Passat looking in the windows. The doors were unlocked. As he made his way to the front of the car, he saw the body of Colin Frye lying in the dirt. Chuck tossed his clipboard to the ground and dropped to his knees next to the body. Rolling Colin onto his back he put his ear to Colin's mouth listening for any signs of life. Colin's breathing was shallow and almost undetectable but he was alive

"My ... wife," Colin whispered.

Chuck looked up from the young man and cringed as he saw Leah. She was impaled against a tree wearing nothing but a bloody t-shirt. Her small feet dangled inches above the wet leafy forest floor. Her head pointed downward with her curly blond hair covering her face. It was obvious to Chuck that she was dead. He returned his focus to Colin. "Stay with me," he said as he reached for his radio.

FIVE

Chuck watched on as the paramedics loaded Colin into the ambulance and sped away, its siren tearing through the quiet morning. Onlookers had gathered in the road and some had even tried to watch from the woods. The police officers had taped off the area as best as they could and told the campers to return to their campsites.

Investigator Stone put his hand under Leah's chin and lifted her head. "Cute girl," he said. He looked down at the steel pole that protruded from her abdomen. "Cause of death is pretty obvious."

Another officer going through a suitcase in the back seat of the car called out to Stone. "He's Colin Frye, twenty-seven, and she's Leah Marx, twenty-four. Looks like they just got married yesterday. His license says Utica, hers says Frankfort."

Another car pulled up; it was Chief Becks. He stepped out of his car and walked past the Passat and into the campsite. "What do we got, Stone?"

"A young female, twenty-four years old, from Frankfort, just married yesterday."

"Looks like someone didn't want her to get married," Becks commented.

"Or someone was in the mood for shish kabob." Stone turned to the crowd and spotted Chuck standing behind the yellow tape. He pointed his finger and then crooked it, signaling him to approach.

Chuck pointed at himself and mouthed the word, *Me?*

Stone nodded his head yes. Most people would have went under the tape, but Chuck was tall enough to step over. He walked up to Stone, who held out his hand.

"Investigator Stone."

Chuck's hand wrapped completely around Stone's palm as he shook it. "Chuck Little," he said. "I'm the head ranger here."

"Little? That's a bit ironic, don't you think?" Stone asked looking up at Chuck. "You play basketball, Chuck?"

"No, do you play miniature golf?" Chuck responded.

"Touché'"

"Who would do something like this?" Chuck asked.

"That's what we're going to find out," Chief Becks assured him.

"When are you going to get her down from there?"

"As soon as the crime scene is finished."

Chuck pointed toward the crowd. "People are taking pictures."

"That's what they do now. In a little while the pictures will be all over Facebook and YouTube," Becks said.

Stone shook his head. "Fucking animals."

SIX

"So you're out of work until the campground re-opens?" Alice inquired.

Chuck sat reading the paper and drinking a cup of coffee. "No, just today and tomorrow. The cops don't want anyone messing with their crime scene. What's for dinner? I'm starving."

"It's only three o'clock. How was she killed?"

"I haven't eaten since breakfast and that was only a couple pieces of toast. We're not supposed to talk about it."

"I can make you a bowl of soup and a sandwich. I'm your wife, and who would I tell?"

"Soup and sandwich would be great. Someone ran a metal stake through her guts and stuck her to a tree."

"That's horrible; I don't think I want to hear anymore."

"You asked," Chuck said, shaking his head.

"Well, forget I asked."

"Where are the boys? I don't want them too far from the house till they catch this guy," Chuck stated.

"Bobby and John are next door, Chucky is upstairs playing in his room."

Alice set the bowl of New England clam chowder in front of her husband and went back to the counter to finish making his sandwich.

SEVEN

"I just got off the phone with the hospital. Colin Frye is going to make it," said Chief Becks, after he hung up the phone.

"I wonder why the killer left him alive," Stone wondered aloud.

"Who knows? Crime scene dusted for prints; hopefully he left one on the stake or maybe touched their car or something."

The phone rang. "Probably another reporter," Stone concluded.

"Go ahead and answer it, and tell them we have nothing to offer them at this time. Tell them as soon as we know something, they will know something."

Stone picked up the phone. "Police station … Yes … No … Not at this time … No … No … Thank you," he hung up and turned to Becks. "We're gonna have to give them something pretty soon."

"Then we better find out something pretty soon."

"I'm waiting to hear back from crime scene, and they're doing an autopsy on the girl this afternoon. Hopefully she fought back and there's DNA under her fingernails. I sent a copy of the report to the state police. They're going to run it through their data base and see if the M.O. matches anything. So for now I guess we just wait."

EIGHT

Harold Burns sat in his recliner in front of the television and as his wife walked through the front door he glanced at his watch and then at her. "It's four o'clock," he said sternly.

"I can tell time." She grinned.

"You think it's funny?" Harold asked.

"What's your problem?"

"Where were you all night?"

"I told you I was going out with friends."

"The bar closes at two. Where did you go after that?"

"I had too much to drink so I rode home with Carol."

"Why didn't she just bring you here?"

"Her house was closer so I just stayed at her house. Christ, why all the questions?"

Harold got up from his chair and grabbed his wife by the arms as she tried to pass.

"Let go of me," she ordered. She looked at her shirt. "Your hands are dirty, look at my shirt now."

"Why are you doing this, Wendy?"

At age forty-seven, Wendy was ten years younger than her husband. She kept long red hair colored to hide any gray that might be sneaking in. She ran, rode her bike, and worked out to keep her body in the great shape it was in. Young men who hit on her in bars usually thought she was in her late thirties. She loved the attention of other men, which had always caused trouble in her marriage. Wendy had been caught twice with other men, both times saying it would never happen again, yet each time Harold forgave her. In the back of his mind however he knew that just because he only caught her twice didn't mean that she had only done it twice.

Wendy pulled loose from her husband's grip. "Doing what__, going out with my friends? You're being stupid. I'm gonna take a sleeping pill and go up and take a nap. I'm tired."

"Do you love me, Wendy?" Harold asked.

"Of course. I'm here, aren't I?"

Harold stood in the middle of the living room and watched as his wife climbed the staircase. He exhaled a long sigh. Confrontations like this usually ended in screaming and yelling, but Harold was exhausted and just wished it would end.

He started to return to the living room until he noticed Wendy's purse on the kitchen table. He listened for the bedroom door to shut and then carefully unzipped the purse. In a small side pocket was his wife's phone. He took it out and slid his finger across the screen. A key pad appeared and he typed in the pass code.

Wendy never worried about leaving her cell phone lying around; she had no idea that Harold new the code. Harold had seen Wendy type it in months ago and had been reading her text messages ever since, and he was smart enough to never let her know what he had read for fear she would change the code. It had always amazed Harold that Wendy thought she was smarter than someone who had spent thirty years on the police force, twenty of which were spent as an investigator.

Harold tapped the message icon. Carol's name was at the top of the list, so he touched her name and the messages appeared.

Wendy: hey wat time did u get home

Carol: around 2:30. u?

Wendy: heading home now

Carol: omg its 5 in the afternoon

Wendy: i didnt want to leave his house.

if Harold asks i slept at ur house last night

Carol: ok

Wendy: breakfast tomorrow morn?

Carol: sure

Wendy: good, got more to tell ya.

Harold pressed the button on top of the phone and the screen went dark, then he placed it back where he had found it and zipped the purse closed.

NINE

The familiar squeal of school bus brakes brought Chuck out of his slumber. The shades were open, but the thick gray clouds didn't allow much sun to shine through the windows. Chuck didn't get much sleep with visions of a young girl nailed to a tree lurking in his brain all night. The last time he remembered looking at the clock on the night stand was 3:15.

He lay in bed on his back with his fingers clasped behind his head. He could hear the sounds of the boys scurrying to gather their things together and get to the bus before it left. Their feet shuffled across a creaking wooden floor, the door slammed twice, and then slammed once again a few seconds later, telling Chuck that someone had forgotten his lunch. He heard his son's feet slapping down the cement walkway to the bus, then the squeak of the door closing, and it pulled away.

A day off with pay, Chuck thought, *what to do, what to do.* He wondered how hard it would be to get Alice back in bed.

"Breakfast is ready," his wife called up the stairs.

Chuck wondered how hard it would be to get her back in bed after breakfast. "I'll be right down," he hollered back.

On his way down the hall to the bathroom he heard the phone ring. He closed the bathroom door behind him and heard his wife yell, "It's for you."

"Take a message."

"He says it's important."

"Who is it?"

"Says his name is Stone."

"Okay, okay, be right there. Christ, a guy can't even take a shit without someone bothering him."

Chuck finished his business, washed his hands, and threw water on his face and through his hair before going to the phone. "Hello."

"Holy shit, Little what the hell took you so long? Have one caught crossways?"

"What is it, Stone? It's my day off, ya know."

"It *was* your day off, Little; we don't have the man power for this kinda thing, so until further notice, you're my new partner."

"Enough manpower for what kind of thing?"

"We got another one," Stone said, his tone instantly serious.

"Another one what?"

"Another body."

Chuck felt the hair on the back of his neck stand up and his mouth go dry. "Wh … where?" he stuttered.

"Limekiln. How quickly can you get here?"

Chuck looked at his wife; she could see in his eyes that something was wrong. "Thirty minutes."

TEN

Chuck gave the young man in the entrance booth a wave as he drove his old white pickup through the gate, trying his hardest to drive slowly. The crime scene wasn't hard to find, Chuck just had to look for the flashing yellow lights and small army of police officers.

Parking his truck at the edge of the road he got out and joined Investigator Stone in front of a young red headed woman who had been pinned to a tree with a steel bar. Just like Leah Marx, her feet were inches from the ground and her head hung downward. The victim wore only a red flannel shirt that was unbuttoned and parted just enough to see the sides of her breasts and a pair of yellow thongs.

"Victim's name is Alison Reed, thirty-four, address on her driver's license is Ellmore Drive in Whitesboro," Stone said.

"Who found her?" Chuck asked.

Stone nodded in the direction of a squad car. "Boyfriend. Says he got a call from work about eleven o'clock last night. He works at a nursing home on Genesee Street. He had accidently brought home some keys from work and they needed them right away. Since it was the only set, he had to drive back down to Whitesboro and then to Utica where he worked. He said he asked his wife to come with him, but she told him she would be fine and for him to just come back up early this morning. When he got here this is what he found."

Chuck scratched his beard. "Jesus Christ."

"The husband called 911 and the state guys responded; of course they called me when someone realized the similarities."

Chuck remembered something. "Van Helsing," he said.

"You got it," Stone agreed.

"Can't be; they put that guy away fifteen years ago. He's in prison."

A young cop, whose name tag read Officer Williams, and who also looked to be about thirteen years old, stepped in front of Stone and Chuck. "Van Helsing, you mean the Dracula guy?"

"That's where they got the name from," Chuck answered.

"I don't get it," Williams stated.

Chuck looked at Stone for approval, and Stone nodded yes. "About fifteen years ago," Chuck began, "we had a few murders, four, I think it was. This guy, Sam Morgan, killed these women around the Old Forge area; he killed them all with handmade steel stakes. That's where the media got the name, *The Van Helsing murders*. First he killed one in her twenties, then one in her thirties, and then forties. The last killing was a woman in her fifties. It all happened over a three-month period of time."

"But they caught the guy, right?" Williams asked.

"They arrested him," Stone replied. "But they didn't have enough to hold him; the evidence just wasn't there. A few weeks after the last murder, Morgan was stopped at a DWI checkpoint outside of Inlet; the officer said Morgan became angry and combative. He was told to pull to the side of the road and when they searched his vehicle they found cocaine. That was enough to charge him with possession and intent to distribute. He went to prison and the murders stopped. The case eventually went cold."

A state trooper walked up to Stone. "We just got a call back from Dannemora; Morgan was released three weeks ago. Good behavior."

"Looks like his behavior went from good to bad real quick," Stone said.

"They gave us his address—an apartment in Utica. We have a car on the way to pick him up," the trooper added. "And guess where he works."

"A nursing home on Genesee Street?" Chuck responded.

The trooper shook his head. "That's right; Saint Joseph's Nursing Home on Genesee Street."

"What a coincidence," Stone said. "And I bet we'll find out he hasn't shown up for work in the last couple of days."

ELEVEN

Harold Burns rinsed his breakfast dishes in the kitchen sink and then went to the couch and folded the blanket he had used the night before. Wendy's sleeping pills had made her sleep through the night, and Harold decided to sleep on the couch, as he did a lot of nights lately. After folding the blanket, he laid it across the back of the couch and then adjusted the pillows. He heard his wife enter the room but he didn't look up.

"Wow, I can't believe I slept through the night like that," Wendy said.

Harold didn't answer. Instead he walked to the kitchen counter, grabbed the coffee pot, and poured himself a cup of steaming black liquid.

"What's your problem?" Wendy asked.

Harold shook his head. "My wife goes out for a couple of drinks and then doesn't come home until the next afternoon."

"I thought we already talked about this."

"No, *you* talked about it on your way through to bed."

"I don't have time for this, Harold."

"I know, you have time to hang out in bars, you have time to go shopping, you have plenty of time to spend with your friends, but you don't have a few minutes to talk to your husband."

"Because it's always the same thing over and over again, you're like a broken record."

"Yeah, I'm the one who's broken."

"Clever, Harold. I gotta go."

"Where are you going now?" Harold asked, trying to control his anger.

"I'm going to have breakfast with Carol."

"Sure you are."

Wendy reached into her purse and pulled out her cell phone. "Call her if you don't believe me."

"Just go," Harold said as he turned and walked back into the living room.

As Wendy went toward the front door she said, "I love you."

"Yeah, sure."

TWELVE

Chuck and Stone stood in front of Chief Beck's desk waiting as he finished up his phone conversation. When he hung up he looked at Stone. "You were right; he hasn't shown up for work in three days. I also got a call back from Utica PD; Williams wasn't home and his neighbors haven't seen him in a few days."

"He could be anywhere," Stone said. "He knows these woods; he lived here most of his life."

"I don't get it," Chuck said. "Last time the killings happened over a few months' time. Why would he kill two nights in a row?"

"Maybe he's in a hurry," Becks said.

"We should talk to Harold Burns," Chuck offered.

Becks looked surprised. "That's a good idea; after all he was the lead investigator the last time."

*****

Stone turned left off of Crosby Boulevard on to Garman Avenue and slowed as he examined the numbers on each house.

"Do you know Harold?" Chuck asked.

"Never met him; he left a week before I started. Why, do you know him?"

"Not really; I met him once. His wife is the social butterfly in that marriage."

"The rumors say it's not much of a marriage. I've heard she'll jump in the sack with any guy who buys her a beer or tells her she's pretty."

Stone pulled his truck to the side of the street; the two men got out and made their way along a dirt path between two concrete forms that had been set in place to pour a new sidewalk that would lead to Harold's front door. Large broken pieces of concrete lay in a pile on the front lawn. Stone carried a large manila envelope in one hand and knocked on the door with the other. The door opened.

Mr. Burns, I'm investigator Sto__,"

"I know who you are," the man gruffly cut him off. "What do you want?"

"Sir, we would like to speak to you about Sam Morgan," Chuck said.

"Sam Morgan," Harold repeated. "Haven't heard that name in a while. Come on in."

All three men sat around the kitchen table drinking coffee. "There's been two murders in the last two days, Burns," Stone said.

Harold slowly shook his head. "The news only mentioned *one* murder."

"There was another this morning," Chuck explained.

"What makes you think it's connected to Sam Morgan?"

Stone opened the envelope and spread four eight-by-ten color photographs of the two victims on the table. "The M.O. is the same, stake through the gut. First victim was in her twenties an__"

"The second was in her thirties," Harold finished. "And I bet you didn't find any fingerprints either, did you?"

"Nothing, not even a partial."

Harold got up from the table, went to a cabinet, and opened a drawer. There were several envelopes in the drawer, and Harold flipped through them until he came to the one he was looking for, pulled it out, and tossed it on the table. "I got a letter from the parole board about four weeks ago saying Morgan was going to be released."

"Has he contacted you?" Chuck asked.

"No, but I kind of expected him to."

"Why?" Stone asked.

"He always said he was innocent, said I planted the coke on him because I didn't have enough to charge him with the murders. When they took him out of the court room he was yelling that he would get even with me some day."

"Did you?" Chuck asked.

"Did I what?"

"Did you plant the coke?"

Harold got up from the table and sauntered to the sink. Dumping out his coffee he said, "I won't justify that with an answer. "Now get out of my house."

THIRTEEN

Stone hung a right on to Route 28. They were halfway through Thendara when Chuck asked, "Where are we going?"

"Utica."

"When are we gonna be back?"

"I don't know. Why, ya got a date?"

"No, but I didn't tell my wife I was gonna be late."

Stone raised one eyebrow and glanced over at Chuck. "Are ya shittin me? She's your wife, not your mother. I don't think she will ground you when you get home, for Chrissakes."

"Expert on marriage, are ya, Stone?" Chuck asked with a sly grin.

"What the fuck is that supposed to mean?"

"Nothing. Just don't you worry about my relationship with *my* wife."

"Fuck you, Little."

The rest of the trip was pretty quiet.

*****

As they drove slowly up Genesee Street Chuck asked, "You know where this place is?"

Stone mumbled, "I never wrote down the address."

"Good, that should help."

"Look it up on your cell phone."

Chuck pulled his phone from his pocket and flipped it open. "How would I go about doing that?"

"You don't have a smart phone?"

"No, I just have this, but it's out of minutes."

"Good, that should help," Stone echoed.

After driving about two miles they arrived at the nursing home. "Here it is," Stone announced. He took a left onto a driveway that led to the parking lot and parked in the front.

Once inside, Stone flashed his badge at the reception desk. "I'm Investigator Stone and this is Ranger Little," he said to the woman behind the desk.

The woman looked at Chuck with a confused expression. "Like a Texas Ranger?" she asked.

"No," Chuck replied. "Like a Forest ranger."

"*Forest* Ranger?" she repeated.

Stone jumped in. "Yeah, you know, like Ranger Smith on Yogi the Bear. 'Hey, Boo Boo.'" The confused look never left her face. "Never mind. We're here to talk to whoever is in charge of maintenance."

"Is this about Kevin Reed's wife?" the woman asked.

"Yes," Chuck replied.

"And you guys think Sam Morgan killed her?" she asked.

"Miss, we just need to ask Sam's supervisor a few questions," Stone said.

"That would be Bill Feeny. I'll page him."

Bill Feeny arrived at the front desk a short while later and escorted Stone and Little to the maintenance room. As Stone asked questions, Chuck scrutinized the room.

"Damn shame about Kevin's wife," Bill said.

"How long did Sam Morgan work here?" Stone asked.

"Just a few weeks; seemed like an okay guy."

"For a murderer," Chuck added.

"Did he make any friends here? Did he talk to anyone in particular?" Stone asked.

"Ya know, mostly he kept to himself ... but I did see him having lunch with Kevin out back at one of the picnic tables a couple times last week."

"And Kevin told him about the camping trip. Who exactly called Kevin about the keys?" Chuck asked.

"It must have been Sam," Bill answered.

"Probably a set up to get Kevin away from the campsite," Stone said.

"Hey, look at this," Chuck called out. He picked up a sharp steel rod off of the work bench. "Look familiar?"

Stone eyed Bill. "What are those used for?"

"We use them when we plant grass or when we don't want anyone to walk in a certain area. We pound them in the ground and wrap that tape from one to the other," Bill answered pointing at a roll of red caution tape hanging on the wall.

"There's a bunch of them here," Chuck said.

Just then Stone's cell phone rang. "Stone here."

"Hey, it's Becks. Where are you?"

"Utica."

"What the hell are ya doing down there? Get your ass back here. They found Morgan's body in the woods near the Bald Mountain trailhead."

FOURTEEN

Stone and Chuck walked through the front doors of the Town of Webb Police Station. "Glad you could make it," Chief Becks announced.

"Sorry, Becks; we just wanted to ask a few questions where Morgan worked."

"We?" Chuck asked.

Stone shot Chuck a look and then focused on Becks. "Who found Morgan's body?"

"Some hikers. M.E. said he's been dead at least four days."

"That's impossible," Chuck proclaimed.

"How did he die?" Stone asked.

"Blunt-force trauma to the back of the skull."

"Don't tell me you two guys are moonlighting as masons now," Becks probed, pointing at the steel rod in Chuck's hand.

"What do you mean?" Chuck asked.

"The pin … in your hand, they're used for setting forms for pouring concrete," Becks clarified.

Stone and Chuck exchanged a look. "How old is Harold Burns' wife?" Stone asked.

Chuck answered, "Gotta be in her late forties. Why do you ask__, oh shit!"

Stone and Chuck headed for the door as Becks grabbed a radio off of his desk.

*****

Stone's black F-150 quietly rolled to a stop in front of the Burns' residence. The two men leapt from the truck and quickly made their way to the front door. Chuck looked down at the scattered steel pins that lay next to the broken concrete as he hurried by.

Stone reached the door first and started to knock just as he heard a scream. He stepped back and drew his weapon. Chuck put his hand on Stone's shoulder and with one swift kick shattered the door jamb and ripped the door from its hinges.

"Move away from her!" Stone hollered as he entered the kitchen.

Burns spun around with a surprised look on his face. Chuck flew by Stone tackling Burns. The two men slid across the hard wooden floor and came to rest against the far wall of the kitchen.

"You're under arrest, asshole," Chuck said, climbing off of Burns.

Stone scrambled over and shoved a knee in Harold Burns' back, and removing his handcuffs from their place on his belt, he said, "Harold Burns, I'm placing you under arrest for the murders of Leah Marx and Alison Reed."

FIFTEEN

Half-way between Whitesboro and Old Forge, along Route 12 South, Chuck turned to Stone and said, "I don't know why I had to come. My wife's pissed at me already for missing dinner; it was shepherd's pie, my favorite."

Stone glanced over. "You'll be home before eleven, so stop bitching."

"Couldn't the Whitesboro P.D. handle this?"

"It's my case."

"Our case," Chuck corrected.

"That's what I meant, our case, and I wanted to be the one to tell Kevin Reed that we got his wife's killer. Besides, it will give us a chance to give him back her personal effects," Stone answered, motioning toward the large white envelope on the seat between them.

Chuck reached over, picked up the envelope, and opened it. He reached in and pulled out a watch, looked at it, and placed it back in the envelope. Then he pulled out her driver's license, read it, and slipped it back inside. He shook the envelope and peered inside and then shook it again before he resealed it and tossed it back on the seat.

"I get that Burns killed the first two women to make it look like the killer had returned after all these years so that when he killed his own wife no one would suspect him, but it seems like a big coincidence that he killed the wife of someone Morgan knew," Chuck said.

"Well, Burns lawyered up, so we couldn't question him tonight, but it'll all come out tomorrow. He'll crack under questioning, they always do, and then he'll try to cut a deal with the D.A."

Chuck shrugged. "I guess."

*****

Stone pulled up in front of the small house on Clinton Street and parked. The two men walked up to the front door and knocked. A few moments later Kevin Reed opened the door.

"Can I help you?" he said.

"I'm Investigator Stone and this is Ranger Little. Can we step inside for a minute? We have your wife's personal effects." Stone held up the envelope.

"I'm kind of in a hurry," Reed said.

Chuck looked confused. "This will only take a second, Reed."

"Of course … yes … what am I thinking? Come in, please."

Stone and Chuck walked through the door into the living room. As Stone told Kevin Reed about the arrest of Harold Burns, Chuck peered around the room. He looked through an open door into a bedroom and noticed an open suitcase lying on the bed.

"Going on a trip, Mr. Reed?" Chuck asked.

"What … oh yes, I just wanted to get out of town for a few days, what with everything that's happened."

Stone noticed two plane tickets laying on the coffee table. "Are you going alone?"

Reed quickly looked down at the tickets. "No, a friend is coming with me."

"Mr. Reed, why wasn't there a wedding ring in your wife's personal effects?" Chuck asked.

"Um … I don't know, maybe she was afraid she would lose it in the woods, maybe."

"Is that what she was afraid of, Kevin?" Stone asked.

"I'm not sure what you mean," Reed answered as he made his way toward the bedroom. "Like I said, gentlemen, I'm in a hurry. I have a plane to catch."

"There was no pocketbook with her things either," Chuck added. "Did she always go away for the weekend without her purse?"

Just then the front door swung open behind Stone and Chuck, and they turned just Reed ran into the bedroom.

"Ready, Kev?" said the young woman walking through the door, suitcase in hand. She paused when she saw the two men standing in the middle of the living room. She started to speak but paused as she saw Kevin re-enter the room. Stone and Chuck quickly spun around; Stone's hand rested on his weapon.

Kevin Reed stood holding a pistol, pointing it at Stone and then at Chuck. "Take your hand off of your gun," Kevin said.

"Not a chance," Stone responded.

"Kevin, put down the gun," the woman yelled.

"They ruined everything," Kevin shouted. "I wanted to be with you."

"Lay down your weapon, Reed," Stone said calmly.

Kevin pointed the gun at Stone, and Chuck rushed him. Kevin fired his weapon as Stone drew his, firing three rounds into Kevin's chest. Kevin stumbled backward and fell on his back. He lay motionless as a puddle of blood pooled underneath him.

The young woman tried to run to Kevin's side, but Stone pushed her back on to the couch. "Stay there and don't move."

Chuck thumped to the floor holding his side, his shirt bloody. "Am I gonna die?" he asked with a frightened tone.

"Probably … when your wife tries to get the bloodstain out of that shirt."

Chuck laughed and then winced in pain. "Don't make me laugh, asshole."

Farmhand

June 6th 1980

"So, are you going out with him?" Monica asked.

Kristen Sawyer slammed her locker door. "I guess. I said I would, and it's tonight. Too late to back out now."

"I think he's cute," said Francine.

Kristen turned and the three girls started down the hall, books in hand.

"Yeah, I guess," Kristen agreed. "He's cute … but kinda dorky."

"Name one boy in our school that's not dorky," Monica said.

"Pat Temple," Kristen answered.

Monica laughed. "Yeah, well, until Pat Temple asks you to the movies, David Cargill will have to do"

"I won't hold my breath," said Kristen. "Seniors don't ask out freshman very often."

"Unless you're Kayla Riddle," Francine pointed out.

"Well I don't do what Kayla Riddle does, so I guess that counts me out."

Monica turned into room 304. "See you guys after school," she said.

Kristen and Francine both said "see ya" and walked another few feet to room 306. They took a seat next to each other, at their desks.

"What movie are you going to see?" Francine asked.

"*Farmhand*," Kristen replied.

"*Farmhand*? Yeah, I hear it's supposed to be pretty scary—though you'd never know it from that stupid title."

"Well, it's either that, The Empire Strikes Back, or something called Urban Cowboy. I don't like westerns."

"I don't think Urban Cowboy is a western, I think it's a love story or something," said Francine. "How are you getting there?"

"His dad is driving us."

Mrs. Grates, their geometry teacher, entered the room. "Okay kids, quiet down, quiet down. Turn you books to page 298, please ..."

*****

"Someone's coming up the driveway!" shouted eight-year-old Mary Sawyer. She ran up the stairs and down the hall to her sister's bedroom. "He's here, Kristen, he's here!"

"Shut up , Mary, and get out of here. Mom!" Kristen sat at her make up table, curling iron in hand. She stared into the mirror, trying her best to get each curl perfect.

Mary stood in the doorway, leaning against the doorjamb, her arms folded in front of her. "Kristen's got a boyfriend, Kristen's got a boyfriend," she sang through a devilish grin.

"Mom! Tell Mary to shut up."

"Mary, leave you sister alone," Grace yelled up the stairs.

Ding-dong!

Richard Sawyer removed his reading glasses and laid them on the end table next to him, folded the newspaper he was reading, and got up to answer the door.

"Good evening, sir," said the boy who had just rang the doorbell. "I'm David Cargill." He looked up at the gentleman standing next to him. "This is my father, Joe Cargill. He said you would probably want to meet him."

Richard shook David's hand and then his father's. "It's nice to meet you both," he said. "I'm Kristen's father, Richard. Please come in." He closed the door behind them and then led them into the living room where he offered them a seat. "Kristen should be down any minute."

David and his father sat down on the couch and Richard returned to his recliner.

David looked around the room nervously. "Beautiful home you have, sir."

"Thank you, David."

"Long driveway," Joe added. "Must be hell to shovel in the winter."

Richard laughed. "A friend of mine plows it for me. Now, you have the hardware store over in Dunquin Cove. Is that right, Joe?"

"Yes, that's right."

"Nice place. Been in there a few times. Your father was also Joe."

"Yes. He retired and moved down to Florida about eight years ago, now."

Richard turned to David. "So what are your plans, son?"

"I plan on going to college after I graduate, sir … for business."

Richard smiled. "I meant this evening, son."

David's face reddened. "Oh. My dad is driving us to the theater in Dover. We're going to see a movie, and afterwards get a bite at the diner down the street from the theater."

"What are you seeing?" Richard asked.

"*Farmhand*."

"*Farmhand*? Never heard of it."

"You and me both," said Joe. "One of those slasher films all the kids are seeing now."

"Slasher film, huh? Sounds very educational," Richard joked. "You going to hang around there in the parking lot till the movie is over, Joe? Or maybe sit through the picture yourself?"

"Lord, no. I'll probably drive home and then go back and pick them up later. It's only about a thirty minute drive."

Just then Kristen walked into the living room, followed by her mother. David quickly stood. "Hi, Kristen," he said, his voice cracking.

"Hi, David," she replied, blushing.

"Grace," Richard said. "This is David Cargill and his father, Joe. Joe owns the hardware store over in Dunquin Cove."

"It's nice to meet you ma'am," said David.

Joe stood. "It's a pleasure to meet you, Grace."

Grace shook David's hand and then his father's. "It's nice to meet you both. Kristen has told us so much about you, David."

"Mo-*ommm*," Kristen scolded.

"Are you ready to go?" David asked.

"Yes."

Richard patted David on the back as they all walked toward the door. "David, my daughter's curfew is usually ten o'clock, but under the circumstances—your father being your escort—we told her she had until eleven."

"Yes, sir, Mr. Sawyer, I'll make sure she is home before eleven."

Joe gave Richard a smile and a wink, and they shook hands one more time.

*****

Joe Cargill pulled the 1979 Monte Carlo to the curb in front of The Strand Theater. "I'll pick you kids up in front of the diner at ten-fifteen, on the dot," he informed them.

"Okay, Dad," said David as he opened the rear, passenger-side door and climbed out onto the sidewalk. He sprinted around the back of the car and gallantly, if clumsily, opened Kristen's door.

"Thank you for the ride, Mr. Cargill," Kristen said before stepping out.

"My pleasure. You kids have fun."

David slammed the car door and his father pulled away from the curb, tooting the horn once as he drove down the street.

"Your Dad seems really nice."

David held the door open for his date and they walked into the crowded lobby. "Yeah, I guess." He reached into his back pocket and pulled out his blue tri-fold wallet with a Velcro fastener. "Two tickets for *Farmhand*," he told the attendant in the glass booth.

"Six bucks," said the guy robotically without looking up.

David ripped open the Velcro and winced at the flatulent sound it made, hoping Kristen hadn't noticed. He removed a ten-dollar bill and handed it to the man, who handed him back the two tickets and his change, all still without looking.

"Thanks. Enjoy the show."

"Well, that guy's Mr. Personality," David commented, breaking the ice as they strolled past the coming attraction posters.

Kristen laughed. "For sure."

"You want popcorn?"

"Sure."

"Soda?"

"Sure."

David ordered a small popcorn with extra butter and two small sodas, then the two of them went into the theater and found a seat in the middle of the room.

*****

After the show David and Kristen walked down the street toward the Landmark Diner. David thought about reaching out and taking her hand, but as this was the first date he had ever been on, he was too nervous.

He held the door once again for Kristen and they took a seat in one of the many booths along the wall, in front of the windows.

A tall thin waitress with her dark hair pulled back into a tight bun walked by with a pot of coffee in her hand. David guessed her to be about fifty years old. She wore a light blue uniform with a white apron. "Coffee?" she asked, in a strong New England accent.

"I'll have a Coke," David said.

"Me too," answered Kristen.

"I'll be right back with those."

"Thanks," the kids said.

David grabbed two of the four laminated menus that were wedged between the napkin holder and the condiment caddie. They both scanned one side of the menu, flipped it over and looked over the other side.

The waitress, whose name tag said ABBY, returned with the sodas and, peering over the top of her cat-like glasses, asked, "What else can I get for you kids?"

"I'll have a cheeseburger and fries, please" David replied.

"I'll just have a small fry," said Kristen.

Abby scribbled the order onto a guest check. "Comin' right up." She turned, walked behind the counter, and slapped the check down onto a 16d nail that had been driven up through a 3/4-inch block of wood. "Order up!"

"So what did you think of the movie?" David asked.

Kristen's eyes widened. "It was really good, but gory."

"I know," David agreed. "When he cut that guy's head off with the sickle and it flew through the air like that, I thought I was going to hurl."

"How about when he stabbed the other guy with the pitch fork? That was so gross."

"It looked so real."

Kristen laughed. "How many people's heads have you seen cut off?"

"None. I hope I never do."

"Me neither," Kristen agreed. "Monica said she heard from someone that when they first showed the movie, people were so scared they had to be carried out of the theater, and they had to cut parts out so it wasn't too scary."

"Wow, that's crazy. I heard that the movie is doing so good that they're already talking about making a sequel."

"Really? That would be cool. We should make a pact. No matter where we are, or what we're doing, we'll see the sequel together."

David smiled and reached across the table. "Shake on it?"

Kristen shook his hand.

June 13th 1981

It was Saturday afternoon, and David Cargill was on his knees in the paint aisle of Cargill Hardware. He ripped open the top of a cardboard box containing four gallons of white ceiling paint, and with his price gun, he put a $5.99 price tag on the lid of each can. After he priced the cans he placed them on the shelf, rotating the older cans to the front, and the newer cans to the rear.

David glanced up at the clock. 4:30; half hour to go.

"Excuse me, David," came a woman's voice from behind him.

David turned and looked up to see Peg O' Leary standing over him. "Hi, Mrs. O' Leary," he said. "How are you today?"

"Good, David. Can you check and see if the shutters my husband ordered came in? Your dad said they were to come in yesterday."

"Sure thing," David said, climbing to his feet. "I think they did. I'll check the store room." David sat the price gun on top of one of the paint cans and walked toward the back of the store.

Peg walked back to the register and leaned against the counter.

"What can I get for you today, Peg?" Joe Cargill asked as he rounded the corner out of the electrical aisle.

"I sent David back to see if my shutters came in."

"They did. Came in yesterday afternoon."

David emerged empty-handed. "I don't see them back there."

"They're behind the steel shelving, Dave," his father called back.

David spun around and went back the way he had come.

"Looks for things about as well as my boy," Peg commented.

Joe chuckled. "The age, I guess."

"Year older than my Monica, isn't he?"

"Sixteen," said Joe. "Be seventeen in December. Just bought himself a car."

"That's scary." Peg remarked. "My boy, Frank Jr., is seventeen. Got his license, no car yet."

"Graduates this year, doesn't he?"

"Yup. First one."

"What's he got planned?"

"Says he's going in the service."

David returned with eight sets of black vinyl shutters and leaned them against the counter. "There's eight more sets," he panted. "I'll be right back."

"I can ring you up now, Peg. Is there anything else?"

"My husband told me to make sure they came with screws."

"Yup. There's a package of screws with each set."

David returned with the rest of the shutters and loaded them in Peg's truck. He slammed the tailgate. "There you go, Mrs. O' Leary."

Peg pulled two dollars out of her pocket book and handed them to David. "Thanks, David."

David put up his hands. "That's not necessary, Mrs. O' Leary."

"You're dad said you just bought a new car. Here, take it. Put it in your gas tank."

David took the money. "Thank you."

As David walked back through the front door he turned and glanced up at the clock over the door.

"Been looking at that clock a lot this afternoon," his father pointed out. "Got a hot date?"

"Me and Kristen are going to see a movie tonight."

Joe opened the register and began counting the money. "What are ya seeing?"

"*Farmhand Two: The Return of Malcolm.*"

Joe thought for a second. "Didn't I take you kids to see one of those movies awhile back?"

"Yeah, it was our first date."

"How long you two been together, now?" Joe asked.

"A little over a year," David answered.

"Wow. Has it been that long?"

*****

David drove his tan 1969 Chevy Caprice up the long driveway to Kristen's house. Kristen looked out the front window when she saw the headlights and waved. David climbed out of the car and walked up the steps, and onto the front porch. Before he had a chance to knock, Mary yanked open the door.

"Hi, David," Mary sang.

David sang back, "Hi, Mary," and walked on by her into the house.

Richard Sawyer was sitting on his La-Z-Boy throne reading the evening newspaper, just like always. He glanced over the top of his reading glasses and said, "Hey, David."

"Hey, Mr. Sawyer," David responded, and took a seat on the sofa across from Richard.

"Seeing a movie tonight?" Richard asked.

"Yes sir."

"How's that car running?"

"Good, sir. Put a new starter in it Thursday night."

"Do that yourself?"

"Yes, sir."

"Good man. There's chocolate chip cookies on the counter in there, if ya want a couple."

David jumped up. "Thank you." As he rounded the corner into the hallway, Kristen met him at the bottom of the stairs.

"Ready when you are," Kristen informed him. "Let me just grab a jacket."

"And let me just grab a couple cookies."

Kristen grabbed her jean jacket and David grabbed his cookies and as they walked out the door, Kristen said, "Bye, Dad. Love you."

"Love you too. Home by eleven please."

*****

David parked two blocks from the theater, and walked around to open Kristen's door. They held hands as they walked along.

"You didn't say much on the ride here," David commented.

Kristen shrugged her shoulders.

"Is everything okay?" David asked.

"Yeah. Everything is fine."

David pulled open the theater door. "It's like deja vu," he said.

Kristen gave him a half smile. "I know. I was surprised you wanted to come to this theater and not the new one in Wells."

"I thought it would be more romantic to come to the same theater."

Kristen cocked her head. "*Farmhand Two* … romantic?"

"Two tickets for *Farmhand Two*."

"Seven and a quarter," the attendant said.

After purchasing the tickets, David walked up to the counter and ordered one large popcorn and two small sodas.

*****

David sat across the booth from his girlfriend at The Landmark Diner. "You know what you want?" he asked.

Kristen scanned the menu. "I think I'm just going to get a BLT."

"That sounds good," David agreed.

"What can I get you kids to drink?" Abby asked.

"I'll have a Coke," Kristen answered.

"Me too, please," said David.

"Do you know what you want to eat, or do you need more time?"

"I'm getting a BLT," Kristen said.

"So am I, and fries."

Abby jotted down the order. "Coming right up," she announced and breezed away, leaving the menthol scent of Bengay in her wake.

David waited for her to get out of earshot and then said, "I think that's the same waitress we had the last time we were here."

Kristen glanced over at her just as Abby shouted, "Order up!"

"I think you're right."

"You think she remembers us?"

"Probably not."

"Should I ask her?"

"No!" Kristen replied. "You know how many customers she's had in the last year or so?"

"I guess you're right. Maybe we should just mention it to her and then see if she remembers us the next time."

"Next time?"

"Who knows, there might be a Farmhand Three."

"What if we're not together when it comes out?"

"What's that supposed to mean?"

"I don't know."

"Then we'll add to the old pact."

"What do you mean?" Kristen asked.

"No matter where we are, no matter if we're together or not, we still have to meet up to see any sequels."

"Sure," Kristen said and stared out the window.

"Here ya go, kids," Abby said, setting their plates in front of them.

"Thank you," Kristen said.

The two finished their sandwiches in complete silence, and David finally tried again. "I know somethings wrong, I can tell. Just tell me what it is."

Kristen let out a long sigh. "Francine told me that Kyle told her that you went and talked to the Air Force recruiter the other day."

"Oh."

"Why did you do that?"

"It's just something I've been thinking about."

"But what about our plans?" Kristen asked. "We talked about going to school in Portland, and getting an apartment together."

"It's not a sure thing. I just talked to them."

"Does your dad know?"

"I haven't told him yet."

"What's he going to say?"

"What can he say? He was in the Navy … and your dad *retired* from the Air Force."

"What about me?"

David reached out and took hold of Kristen's hands. "I just talked to them, that's all."

January 15th 1983

Kristen lay on her back in her canopy bed. It was eight o'clock on Saturday morning and she was already showered and dressed. She had her phone up to her ear.

"What time does his plane get in?" came Monica O' Leary's eager voice from the earpiece.

"He arrives in Portland at 10:05," Kristen answered.

"Are you excited?"

"Yes."

"How long has it been since you seen him?"

"Four months, when I went with his parents to Texas to watch him graduate from basic training."

"You're riding to the airport with his parents?"

"Yeah, they should be here any minute."

"How long is he here for?"

"He's flying back to Maryland on Tuesday morning; he has to work that night at eleven."

"Not much time," Monica pointed out.

"I'm going down in April for a week during spring break."

"Your parents are letting you go?"

"They don't know yet."

"So, what do you have planned for the next three days?"

"We're going to the movies tonight, and then tomorrow he reserved a hotel room in Portsmouth; I'm going to tell my parents he's taking me shopping for the day."

"Ooh, bad girl."

"Ha-ha. It's been so long."

"Kristen, the Cargill's are here!" Grace, her mother, yelled up the stairs.

"I gotta go, Monica. I'll talk to you later."

*****

Kristen stood with Joe and Kathy Cargill in the waiting area, eagerly awaiting David's arrival. Joe Cargill put his arm around his wife; a couple tears were already streaming down her face.

"It's only been a few months," Joe told her.

"That's the longest I've ever gone without seeing him," she explained, wiping a tear from her cheek.

Joe looked down at Kristen. "You're not crying too, are ya?"

"Not yet," Kristen answered.

Joe glanced at his watch. "Hope he gets here soon. It's Saturday, he has to work at the store."

Kristen shot him a horrified look.

"*Just* kidding."

As soon as Kristen looked back in the direction of the arriving passengers her eyes immediately found her boyfriend, and she took off running. When she reached David, she jumped into the air and landed in his arms, her legs wrapped tightly around his waist, and her arms around his neck. She kissed his cheeks, forehead, and lips repeatedly.

"I missed you so much," she whispered in his ear.

"I missed you too. I love you."

"I love you."

Kristen unwrapped her legs and dropped to the floor as Joe and Kathy reached their boy.

"I'm going to need a hug too," Kathy said.

David hugged his mother and then his father.

"How was your flight?" Joe asked. He reached down and picked up David's suitcase.

"Good," said David.

As David walked by his father, Joe turned and put his arm around the young man. "It's great to have you home. You have no idea how proud it makes me to see you in that uniform." Joe choked on the last few words.

"Thanks, Dad," David said, as he reached over and took hold of his girlfriend's hand.

"You hungry?" Kathy asked.

"Starving."

"We'll grab something to eat before we head home," Joe said.

*****

David sat on the sofa across from Richard Sawyer. "So, how's the service treating you, son?"

"Good, sir."

"Kristen tells us you're working in communications."

"That's right, sir."

"Think you might make a career of it?"

"I don't know, too early to tell. I guess if I could stay where I am I wouldn't mind staying in for a while."

"Liking where you are is important, I guess. I have to say, though, I was never stationed anywhere I didn't like."

"You were at Hanscom for a while."

"The last eight years," Richard replied. "Drove from here to there every day for the last three."

Kristen entered the living room, zipping up her coat. "Ready?" she asked.

"Ready when you are."

"David," Grace hollered from the kitchen.

"Yes, Mrs. Sawyer?"

Grace walked into the living room. "We wanted you to come for dinner tomorrow evening."

He glanced over at Kristen. "Um … I, uh … we—"

"We were going into Portsmouth tomorrow to shop and have dinner, Mom," Kristen supplied.

"Well, why don't you just come back here after you shop and have dinner here?"

"Mom, we want to have dinner in Portsmouth."

"What are you going to have in Portsmouth that I can't make you here?"

"Grace," Richard cut in, "the kids want to spend some time alone, for God's sake."

"Okay, okay," Grace said, heading back into the kitchen. "Maybe next time you're in town."

Richard rolled his eyes and grabbed his newspaper off the end table. "Have fun kids. Drive careful."

"Thanks, Daddy," Kristen said, and out the door they went.

*****

Kristen glanced up at the marquee as they drove by the theater. "*Farmhand Three: The Curse of Malcolm,*" she read. "Can you believe it?"

"How many of these movies do you think they'll make?" asked David.

Kristen scooted closer to her boyfriend. "A hundred, I hope."

"Two for Farmhand," David said.

"Eight bucks," said the kid behind the glass.

David handed him a fifty and waited for his change.

"Enjoy the show."

David and Kristen walked through the lobby and up to the concession counter. "There's hardly anybody here," he commented.

"Everyone probably goes to the mall now," Kristen surmised.

David ordered a large popcorn and two medium sodas. "That's too bad. But good for us."

"Why, Mr. Cargill, you wouldn't be thinking of trying to take advantage of little old me in the dark, now would you?" said Kristen coquettishly.

David grinned. "Since when could you read my mind?"

*****

David held open the glass door of the Landmark Diner and the couple took their seats at the usual booth.

"What can I get you kids to drink?" Abby asked.

David and Kristen both smiled.

"I'll have a Coke," David said.

"Me too," said Kristen. "And a BLT."

"Make that two BLTs, Abby, and an order of French fries."

"Coming right up," she said. She went to the window and handed the order to the cook.

"Wonder why they don't use the nail anymore?" David asked.

"Maybe someone hurt themselves with it," Kristen answered. "It looked pretty dangerous."

"You think she takes that bun out of her hair when she goes home at night?"

"This place is open twenty-four hours. You think she even *goes* home at night?"

David laughed. "I wonder."

When Abby returned to the table with their plates, David said, "Can I ask you something, Abby?"

Abby sat their plates in front of them. "Shoot."

"We've been in here twice, before tonight; once in eighty, and once in eighty-one. You were our waitress both times. Do you remember us?"

Abby stared at David for a second and then at Kristen. "Can't say I do." She looked back at David and asked, "Are you tellin' me you only bring your girl out for dinner once a year?"

David took a sip of his soda. "No, that's not it. You ever heard of the Farmhand movies?"

"That crazy farmer that cuts off people's heads with a sickle?"

David chuckled. "Yeah, that's the one."

"What about him?"

"We made a pact years ago that we—Kristen and me—would return here to watch the movie and have dinner every time they made a sequel."

"And there's been three of them so far," Abby said.

"Exactly."

"There gonna be a fourth?" Abby asked.

"Don't know."

"She's Kristen. What's your name?"

"David."

"David and Kristen. If they make another movie I'll try and remember ya. Enjoy your dinner." With that, Abbey sailed away on a Bengay breeze.

June 14th 1985

David Cargill and his father stood in the plumbing aisle of Cargill Hardware. Each had a small, open cardboard box in his hand. The boxes contained 1/2-inch copper fittings, and the two men were dropping them, one at a time, into the proper bins.

"You're heading back on Sunday?" Joe asked.

"Yeah. I have to be back to work on Monday."

"How do you like living off base?"

"I like it a lot better," David replied. "I don't have to pay for a hotel now when Kristen visits."

"She come down quite a bit?"

"She came down for the three-day weekend in May and she visited for a week during her winter break."

"That's nice," Joe said, and dumped the remainder of his box into the bin. "I know you were both worried about the long distance thing. It's good that you can make it work. What are your plans for the weekend?"

"Seeing a movie tonight."

"Oh, that's right. Your mother said tonight was slasher flick number four. What's this one called?"

David grinned. "*Farmhand Four: Farmer Takes a Wife*."

Joe laughed out loud. "Oh my God. What will they think of next? I guess this means there might soon be a bunch of little farmhands running around."

"One can only hope," David joked.

Joe bent over, sat the box on the floor, and picked up another one. He leaned against the rack, took a deep breath, and let it out slowly.

"You alright?" David asked.

Joe ripped open the top of the box. "Yeah, I'm fine," he answered. "Just don't seem to have the pep I used to. Probably just getting old."

"You're only forty-four, Dad. Maybe you should have Mom make you an appointment to see the doctor."

"I have my yearly check-up on Wednesday. I'm sure I'll live till then. What time are you picking up Kristen?"

"She's picking *me* up at five." David glanced up at the clock. "Should be here any minute."

Joe sat his box down on a shelf. "Yeah, I better start closing up. Your mother said not to be late. I guess we're having dinner tonight at The Cove with the Polinowskis."

"Sounds fun," David remarked.

"I guess," his father half-heartedly agreed. "That damn Marvin has a complaint and sends his meal back almost every time we go somewhere to eat with them."

David was still laughing when Kristen walked through the door. "What are you two laughing about?" she asked.

"Some friends of my parents," David explained. "The guy is the crankiest person you ever met in your life."

Kristen gave David a kiss on the lips and then turned to hug Joe. "How have you been, Mr. Cargill?"

"Good, Kristen. How's your parents doing?"

"They're doing good. They get back from Florida on Monday. Stayed an extra month this time."

"I'm surprised they haven't just moved down there permanently."

"They probably will after Mary graduates high school."

"What grade is she in now?"

"She's a sophomore," Kristen answered, and then turned to David. "You ready?"

"I'm ready. You need any help closing up, Dad?"

"Nope. You kids get out of here."

*****

David and Kristen walked out of the theater after the show and strolled down the sidewalk, arm in arm, toward the Landmark Diner.

"I think that was the best one yet," Kristen commented.

"I think you're right," David agreed. "But ten bucks to see a movie is getting a little ridiculous."

David pulled open the door of the diner and Kristen went inside. They took a seat at their usual booth.

"What can I get you kids to—David and Karen," Abby said, pointing her finger from one to the other.

"David and Kristen," said David.

"David and Kristen," Abby repeated. "I was close. *Friday the 13th. Part Four*?"

"*Farmhand Four*," Kristen said.

"Ah, yes. So tell me, what's the old Farmhand up to these days?"

"Well," David began, "he cut off a farmer's head and stole his daughter. Then he tried to convince the daughter to marry him."

"But she didn't want any part of it," Kristen added.

"She probably saw the first three movies," Abby kidded.

"No, she married him," said Kristen. "But it didn't end well."

"I don't even want to know. Two BLTs, two Cokes, and an order of fries?

"Sounds good to me," David said.

"Me too," said Kristen.

August 15th 1986

David Cargill was locking the front door of the hardware store when Howard Tanner pulled up in his van and climbed out. "Am I too late?" he asked over the hood of the van.

"I was just locking up, Mr. Tanner," David answered. "What did you need?"

"The florescent light bulb blew out in the sign over the bakery and I don't have another one."

David unlocked the door. "Come on in, we'll get you one."

Howard shoved the van door closed and followed David into the store. "Thanks a lot, Dave. If I didn't get this bulb in tonight I would hear it from Lita all night."

"No problem, Mr. Tanner. You know how many watts it was?"

"Forty. It's one of the short ones."

David walked down the aisle reading the wattage of each bulb. "Here we go." He removed the bulb from the shelf and handed it to Howard. "Register's closed. I'll have to get you next time."

"Thanks, David, and … I'm really sorry about your father. He was a great guy."

"Thanks, Mr. Tanner. It's been a rough couple of months. We're really going to miss him."

"How's your mom doing?"

"Better than she was. She tries to keep herself as busy as she can. Well, you know, she's here most days."

"I heard you might be coming home to stay."

"Yeah. I turned in my discharge papers. I get out next month."

"Gonna work here at the store?"

"For a while. My mom talked about selling the place, but we'll see."

David and Howard walked out the front door. David locked up and Howard jumped back in his van, waved, and tapped the horn once as he pulled away. Just like David's dad used to do.

*****

"You want me to make you something to eat before you go?" Kathy Cargill asked her son.

David sat on the couch in the living room, bent over as he tied his sneakers. He looked up at his mother standing in the doorway. "We're going to get something to eat after the movie, thanks."

"Okay," said Kathy, her voice little more than a whisper.

David didn't like seeing his mother like this; ten pounds thinner, moving slower. The sadness in her eyes these days was almost more than David could stand. He asked himself at least a hundred times a day, why did this have to happen? A heart attack at forty-five years old was just too young. He missed his father so much, but he knew his mother missed him even more.

David got up from the couch and gave his mother a hug. "I love you," he said. He could feel bones in her back that he had never felt before. It seemed as though he was hugging an old woman, not his mother.

"I love you, too," David. "I'm glad you're moving home."

"Me too, Mom."

*****

David drove his father's black 1982 Ford F-150 up the Sawyers' long driveway. When he pulled up to the house, he left the engine running and beeped the horn.

After a few minutes, Kristen exited the house and climbed into the truck. "You didn't want to come in?" she asked.

"No. I knew if I came in they would probably bring up my father and I didn't feel like talking about him, the store, or anything else."

Kristen put her hand on David's lap. "They care about you."

"I know, but I just don't want to think about it tonight. I just want to relax, see a movie, and get something to eat."

The ride to the theater was quiet. David stared out the windshield at the road ahead and Kristen gazed out the passenger-side window most of the way. When they drove past the theater, Kristen read the marquee. *Farmhand Five: The Spawn of Malcolm*. She made no comment.

"Two for *Farmhand*," David said.

"That'll be ten dollars," said the old gray haired man behind the glass.

David paid and together they walked into the theater.

After the movie, the walk to the diner was just as quiet as the ride to the theater. They sat in their usual booth and ordered their usual meal.

Abby was working behind the counter for the evening, but came out from behind it just to wait on the familiar couple. They talked about the movie for a bit and it was the only time during the night that David felt a sense of normalcy. Seeing Abby was like seeing an old friend, a friend that knew nothing about what he was going through.

*****

At the end of the evening, David drove back up the Sawyers' driveway. He came to a stop and shut off the engine. Kristen didn't move.

"You want me to come in?" David asked.

"No," Kristen answered.

"No? Why not?"

"David, we have to talk."

David took a deep breath and exhaled. "Do we?"

Kristen turned toward him. "I know this is bad timing, and I wanted to tell you last month."

David could tell by the look in her eyes what was coming next, but he asked anyway. "Tell me what?"

"I don't know how to say it."

David just stared at her.

Kristen could no longer look him in the eye; she glanced down at a Coke stain in the truck's striped bench seat. "I've been seeing someone else."

David's heart was pounding and his mouth was instantly dry, "Why?" was all he could think to ask.

"We hardly ever see each other."

"I'm moving home next month."

"I know, but—"

"But it's too late."

Kristen shook her head yes. "I'm sorry."

"Me too," David said.

Kristen kissed him quickly on the cheek. A moment later he watched her disappear through the front door.

October 31st 1989

David Cargill stood behind the checkout counter at Cargill Hardware. He reached into a giant plastic jack-o' lantern and pulled out three miniature candy bars. "Here ya go," he said as he dropped them, one by one, into the yawning sacks of Darth Vader, Spider-Man, and Count Dracula.

"Thank you, Mr. Cargill," the children said in unison.

"You're welcome. Try not to scare anyone too badly tonight."

The kids giggled as they scooted out onto the sidewalk to continue tricking and treating.

David glanced up at the clock over the door. *Hour to go*, he thought, and turned to finish pricing the packages of light bulbs that sat on the counter behind him.

The front door swung open again, and David quickly turned to reach into the candy bucket. "Trick or treat," said a deep voice.

David looked up. "Hey, John. I thought you were more kids," he said.

"I am," John remarked and grabbed four Milky Ways from the pumpkin head in his huge meaty fist.

"What are you doing tonight?" David asked.

"Me and Monica's going to see that new Farmhand movie. There's a midnight showing at that old theater in Dover. You should come with us." John unwrapped all four chocolate bars and shoved them into his mouth.

"No, thanks. I wouldn't want to be a third wheel."

"You wouldn't be. Francine Willis is coming too."

"Oh, is she? This doesn't sound like a setup at all."

"I know I haven't lived here long, man, but we've become pretty good friends. And I'm the kind of guy who likes to see his friends happy."

"What the hell is that supposed to mean?"

John chuckled. "From what Monica tells me, Francine Willis wants to *make* you happy … if ya know what I mean." John gave him a wink.

"What exactly did Francine say?"

John reached into his shirt pocket. "She gave me this note to give you. She wants you to check yes or no."

David cocked his head. "Really?"

John's empty hand came back out of his pocket. "No, not really. She just said she has always liked you and she wants you to come to the movies with us. How about it?"

David sighed. "I guess."

"Good," John said. "But try to look a little more excited when you see her."

"I'll do my best."

John headed toward the door. "We'll pick you up at ten."

*****

David shoveled the last bite of mashed potatoes into his mouth and swallowed. "That was fantastic, Mom," he said as he pushed the empty plate toward the middle of the table.

"I do my best," she replied. "I hear you have a date tonight."

David gave her a surprised look. "Where the *heck* did you hear that?"

"It's a small town."

"I realize that, but it's only been forty-five minutes since *I* found out I had a date."

Kathy got up from the table and grabbed David's empty plate and glass. "That's odd," she said. "Because I found out about it yesterday."

David left the table and walked into the living room. "Where's the newspaper?" he called out to his mother. "I wanted to have a look at the ad I put in for the store."

"It should be right their next to your dad's chair."

He grabbed the paper off the end table and stared at the La-Z-Boy. After a few seconds he began flipping through the pages of the Dunquin Crier. When he got to the full-page ad, he inspected and mentally approved it, and took it into the kitchen.

"What do you think?" he asked, holding the paper up to his mother.

Kathy scanned the ad. "Very nice."

"Yeah, turned out pretty good. My own layout." David sat back down at the dining room table with the newspaper in front of him. "Any word from Grandpa?"

"His plane leaves Orlando Friday morning. I have to pick him up in Portland at four that afternoon."

"I can't imagine him moving back here."

"With your grandmother gone, he wants to be close to family."

"Family? There's only two of us."

"He's *only* sixty-six years old. He's still young enough to see *your* kids grow up, if you would get on the ball and have some."

"Sorry I'm not moving fast enough."

"You know, David, Francine Willis comes from a big family."

"It's one date, Mom."

*****

Even though David was on a date with Francine, there was a part of him that hoped Kristen would be waiting out front of the Strand Theater when he arrived. It had been a little over nine years since their first date, and that's all he could think about the whole way. Francine tried her best to make conversation, and David tried his best to listen.

John Morgan took a left onto Third Street and as they passed in front of the theater he said, in his scariest voice, "*Farmhand Six: You Reaper What You Sow*. Ooooh, scary."

Monica giggled, the same way she did at almost everything John said.

David looked over at Francine. "Do you like scary movies?"

"Yes," she said. "As long as I have someone to hold onto."

John pulled to the curb across the street from the Landmark Diner.

David glanced over and saw Abby through the window. She was taking an order. It was eleven o'clock, and he thought back to the night he and Kristen wondered if she ever went home at night. He smiled to himself. *Maybe she really doesn't*, he thought. Something inside him made him want to go inside and explain to her what had happened. He wondered if she knew the new *Farmhand* movie was out, and if she would be expecting them. He climbed out of the car and Francine followed.

When the group reached the theater, David pulled open the door and the others went inside. David paused, took one last look around, and followed them in.

June 14th 1991

Joe Cargill Sr. stood on a wooden six-foot step ladder in front of the entrance door of Cargill Hardware. He had pulled the clock off the wall and was inspecting the back of it. He wiggled the cord that ran from the clock into a small hole in the wall, then looked at the face of the clock. He tapped on the plastic lens that covered the face. "Goddamn thing," he grumbled to himself.

"Grandpa, get off that ladder," David scolded as he exited the storeroom. "How many times have I asked you not to do that?"

Joe placed the clock back on its bracket. "You've told me enough times to know that I'm not gonna listen." He climbed down off the ladder, folded it, and placed it against the wall beside the door. "I'm gonna order a new clock."

"You do that."

Joe walked behind the counter, grabbed a catalog, and began flipping through the pages. "Your dad put that clock up there in 1954."

"I know," said David. He had heard the story twenty times before—from his grandfather when he was little, then from his dad, and now from his grandfather again.

Joe went on. "He worked here after school nights and on weekends."

David leaned back against the counter. "Uh-huh," he nodded.

"I was showing him how to do electrical work—you know, small stuff. I was back in the stock room. Your father decides to hook up the new clock. He shuts off the breaker that says clock, not realizing it was the breaker for the old clock."

"Uh-huh."

"Just as I come out of that stock room, he grabs those two wires. Knocked that boy right on his ass. Well, I couldn't quit laughing."

David grinned from ear to ear. "He didn't come back to the store for three days, did he?"

The smiles left their faces at the same time. They were silent for a few seconds and then Joe said, "He was a good man, your dad. You remind me a lot of him."

"You remind me a lot of him too, Grandpa. I'm glad you moved back."

"Me too, boy, me too," Joe said, and buried his face in the catalog.

David was in the plumbing aisle when he heard the phone ring, and a few seconds later he heard Joe call out, "Phone's for you, David."

"I'll get it back here, Gramp."

Joe hit the hold button and laid the phone back in its cradle.

"Hello?" David said.

"It's the final chapter," said a strange, unfamiliar voice.

"Excuse me?"

"*Farmhand: The Final Chapter.* It starts tonight."

"Kristen? Is that you?"

"Fooled you, didn't I? How have you been?"

"Good. How have you been?"

"Good."

"So, what's up?" David asked.

"I'm in town. My plane got in last night," Kristen explained. "I'm just here for the weekend."

"Oh?"

"I was wondering if you wanted to see the movie."

"You missed the last one."

"I saw it in Los Angeles ... by myself. It wasn't the same. I miss you, David."

"I miss you too."

"Do you want to go?"

David was silent for a bit, and then said. "I'll pick you up at seven."

*****

On the way to Dover, David talked about his mother and his grandfather. He talked about the hardware store, too, and anything else he thought she might be interested in.

Kristen talked about her parents and how they were finally moving down to Florida. She talked about her job, and about California. She explained that this would probably be her last visit to the area since her parents were moving away, and the fact that her sister, Mary, now lived in Boston.

David parked his truck in front of the Landmark Diner. He got out, and as he walked around to the passenger side he glanced over, but there was no sign of Abby. The lights were off and a closed sign hung on the door.

He opened the passenger door, and Kristen held out her hand. David helped her out of the truck. He hadn't seen her in almost five years, and she was more beautiful than ever.

"California must really agree with you," David said.

Kristen had moved to Los Angeles right after college and took a job as an administrator in a large nursing home. Twice in the last few years David had heard that she was home to visit, but he didn't see her, and she made no attempt to contact him.

David opened the entrance door for Kristen and followed her inside. "Two tickets for *Farmhand*," he said.

"Twelve dollars," the attendant said. David paid, and together they walked up to the concession stand. "Medium popcorn and two small Cokes."

Kristen looked around the lobby. "Are we the only ones here?" she asked.

"There's a few couples already went in," the woman behind the counter said. "They're tearing the old place down in a couple months."

"Wow, really?" David said. "That's too bad."

Kristen and David walked through the door for the last time and took a seats in the middle of the theater. There were only a few other couples.

Kristen spotted a couple in their mid-teens and jabbed David in the ribs. "Look," she said. "I wonder if it's their first date.

As the lights dimmed, David turned to Kristen and said, "I've asked Francine to marry me."

"I know," said Kristen.

"I told her all about tonight."

"I figured. I just wanted to see you one last time. I wanted to say I was sorry about the way things ended."

"I know."

"Shhh!" someone behind them said

More Questions than Answers

It was early March and Carl Reed was running up US-1, his blue and white Under Armour running shoes sending up a puff of dust with every step. A lizard caught his eye as it scampered across his wife's path just a few feet ahead. It paused to watch them as they ran by and then squeezed under a railroad tie.

"Did you see that?" he asked.

"See what?" she answered.

"A lizard. It ran right in front of you." It was difficult to speak as he ran because it was early in the year and he was not in shape yet. They didn't run in the winter because it was just too cold where they lived, in upstate New York. He and his wife usually started running around the *end* of April but because they were in Key Largo and it was really warm they figured they would give it a go this morning.

"No, I didn't see it. I probably would have screamed."

He laughed.

As they neared their hotel they bared left down Ocean Bay Drive and ran past the Burger King. Carl remembered the fish sandwich, large fries, and coke he had ate at nine the night before. *That was stupid to eat that late*, he thought.

"How much farther do you want to run?" Carl asked, hoping Sandy would say, "This is good." She didn't.

"The end of the road is good."

He focused on the gate at the end of the road. *Thank God, only a few more blocks*. He wiped the sweat from his brow for the fourth or fifth time, he couldn't remember. He just knew it was a lot more times than he would have wiped his forehead if he were running in Herkimer, New York.

Sandy got to the gate first and slowed to a walk. Carl was by her side a few seconds later.

"Wow! It's hot," she blurted out.

"Feels good though … to sweat I mean. I *was* having a hard time breathing. Just not used to this kind of heat I guess."

They turned and starting making their way back the way they had come. When they came to the first street he said, "Let's walk down here." She followed looking at the houses and plants as she walked along.

They took a left onto Point Pleasant Drive. "Look at all of the palm trees," she said. "Do you think they just grow there or do you think someone planted them?"

"I wonder," he answered.

They walked on a little farther and he reached into his pocket for his cell phone. Tapping the camera icon and then pointing the cell at the tall bushes with big red flowers he snapped a picture. "I wonder what these are?" he asked.

"I don't know. They're beautiful, though," she answered.

He wiped his brow again and then grabbed the bottom of his T-shirt with both hands. He fanned it out and in, quickly, over and over again, trying to get it to air dry. The humidity wouldn't allow it.

He snapped a picture of a stucco covered cement block wall that had been painted white once long ago but was now peeling and showing its age. The fine cracks showed exactly where the block's bond lines were. "I wonder how deep you have to go with the footer for these block walls," he pondered. "At home you have to go three feet deep."

"Huh," she responded, trying to show some interest in block wall construction as she gazed out between two of the houses at the water of the Gulf of Mexico. "Just look at the color of that water."

"Do you think the boats at those docks are owned by the people who live in these houses?" he wondered aloud.

She shrugged her shoulders.

Up the road a ways there was a thin man in faded cut-off jeans and a white tank-top, his long graying hair was pulled back into a pony-tail. The man jabbed a long steel pinch bar into a hole in the ground. He lifted the bar into the air, his long lean darkly-tanned arms tightened, and he stabbed it into the hole again with all of his might. He wiggled the bar back and forth loosening the earth at the bottom of the hole.

As Carl and Sandy neared, the man leaned the bar against the white picket fence behind him and then returned his attention to the hole. He pulled a rag from his back pocket and mopped the sweat from his face. As he replaced the rag the approaching strangers caught his eye.

The thin man smiled and said, "I can think of a lot better things I would rather be doing."

Carl and Sandy let out a half-laugh.

"It's a hot one," Carl said.

"You got that right," the thin man agreed.

Carl stopped beside the worker. "Putting up a new mailbox?" he asked, knowing that that's exactly what the man was doing.

The thin man gestured toward the old mailbox just two feet away. "Yeah, the old post is rotted."

Carl made his best attempt to start a conversation as Sandy looked on. "Is this what you do?" Carl asked. "I mean … home repairs."

The thin man motioned back toward the house behind him. "I work for this guy … and then I also work over at the yacht club seven days a week."

"You live right here in Key Largo?"

"Yup … for twenty years now."

"That's awesome," Carl said. "I can't imagine living here."

The man smiled as though he had heard it before.

"It's so beautiful," Sandy added.

Carl thought for a minute. "Hey, how deep do you have to go with a footer for one of these block walls?"

"Not far, maybe a few inches."

"You would have to go three feet deep, where we live, to get below the frost line."

The thin man laughed. "Well, yeah, we don't have to worry about that here."

Carl smiled. "I guess not."

"Where are you from?" the thin man asked.

"Upstate New York ... on the thruway between Albany and Syracuse. A little bit colder there."

"Oh, I know all about the cold. I lived in Minnesota for the first thirty years of my life. Then I came down here for a visit and never left. Been here for twenty years now."

"It seems like nobody who lives here is from here," Carl pointed out.

"That's the truth," the thin man agreed.

Carl pointed at the house behind the thin man. "How much a house like this go for?"

The thin man looked into the air for the answer. "Around three million, probably."

"Wow," Carl said. "A house like that back home would sell for around two hundred and twenty thousand."

The thin man pointed at another smaller building on the same property. "He also has that small apartment there and there's a pool around back. This place belongs to Jim Benz." The thin man paused for a moment waiting for a reaction as though Carl and Sandy must have heard of Jim Benz. When there was no reaction he continued, pointing over Carl's shoulder. "Jim Benz ... he owed the refrigeration place over here. Sold that building. He also has a place up in Miami. He'll fly down here in his helicopter. I'm always nervous when I watch him land ... always think he's gonna go right into the pool."

"Oh my God!" Sandy said, imagining Jim Benz's helicopter crashing into the pool.

Carl chuckled at the story.

The thin man reached back and grabbed his steel bar. Carl took it as a sign that he was ready to get back to work.

"Well, we better keep moving," Carl said.

"Yeah, I better get back to work," the thin man agreed.

Sandy gave a little smile and a wave and started walking down Point Pleasant Drive. Carl caught up to her and they turned the corner onto Bayview Drive.

Sandy pointed at the bushes that were hanging over a wooden fence. "Hey, look, there's more of those same bushes but with a different color flower."

"I wonder what they are called."

"You should have asked that guy."

"Yeah, I should have. Well, at least I know how deep to pour a footer."

A Genius Plan

An Adirondack Short Story

Chuck Little maneuvered his long leg out from under the blanket, trying to get some relief from the record high July heat, then he flipped his pillow over hoping the other side was cooler. The ceiling fan slowly revolving above his head was not doing its job. He opened one eye and glanced over at the other side of the bed. Alice wasn't there. She had gotten up two hours earlier when Chuck Jr. entered the room saying he had to puke. He breathed in slowly through his nose hoping for the aroma of frying bacon, but there was none.

Chuck reached up with his long, orangutan-like arms and pulled the fan chain two clicks, bringing it up to the high-speed setting. He dropped back onto his pillow and shut his eyes. A car horn out front honked and Chuck flipped over onto his stomach.

The fan was now turning just fast enough to make the fan chain and light chain hit together every two seconds. *Tick, tick, tick, tick.* "Sonofabitch," Chuck grumbled. He reached up and pulled the chain two more times, bringing it back to its original speed, and then the alarm clock went off. Chuck stared at the old digital clock, shaking his head slowly.

A car alarm began bleating and Chuck climbed out of bed. He went to the alarm clock and shut it off. He grabbed a hair tie off the dresser, pulled his long hair back into a ponytail, and secured it with the tie, and then made his way over to the bedroom window, which overlooked the street, and pulled back the curtain.

A bald fat man wearing denim carpenter shorts and a red tank top was pointing his key fob at his gray Ford Taurus trying to turn off the alarm. On the tenth or eleventh try he succeeded, turned, and began walking down the street.

"Goddammit," Chuck whispered and pulled down the top sash of the window. "You're parked halfway in my driveway!" he shouted.

The man turned back toward the house and Chuck pointed at the Taurus. The man smiled, waved, and went on his way. Chuck slammed the window shut and then raised the bottom sash, hoping it would let in some cooler air.

After putting on his robe, he walked down the hall toward the bathroom. First he passed Bobby and John's room. They were both in bed, still asleep. Then he came to Chuck Jr.'s room.

Chucky was lying in bed with his eyes open. A large, orange plastic bowl—the puke bucket, it had been named in recent years—was sitting on the floor next to his bed.

"How ya feelin', buddy?" Chuck asked his six-year-old son.

Chucky shrugged his shoulders.

"Any better?" asked Chuck.

"A little," Chucky answered. "My head hurts." No sooner did Chucky get the words out of his mouth than, he vomited, completely missing the bowl. He wiped his mouth with his pajama sleeve and laid back. "I feel better now."

"That's good," Chuck responded, and then shouted down the stairs. "Alice! Chucky needs you!" Chuck walked into the bathroom and closed the door behind him. He took off his robe, threw it over the edge of the bathtub, pulled down his boxers and sat on the toilet. He reached down beside the toilet for a magazine and knocked something off of the magazine rack. *What's this?* he thought, and picked it up. It was an early pregnancy test stick and in one of the two windows was a small blue plus sign. Chuck looked up toward the heavens. *Why ... why?*

*****

The second Investigator Eric Stone walked through the front doors of the Town of Webb Police Department, Chief Becks threw open his office door. "Stone, we got another break-in." Becks glanced down at the yellow Post-It note in his hand. "129 Riverside Drive. There's a unit there now."

Stone snatched the note from Becks' hand and stuck it to his own forehead with a *smack*. "Same as the last three?" he asked, as he made his way to a small table against the wall containing an open box of muffins and an old Mr. Coffee coffee machine.

"Same but different," Becks replied.

Stone poured himself a cup of coffee into a Styrofoam to-go cup. "Muffins? Who brought in muffins? What do you mean, same but different?"

"They killed the homeowners' two dogs."

"Jesus Christ. Smashed up the last place and now the bastards have killed two dogs. Sounds like things are escalating."

"Got away with it the first few times. Now their confidence is growing."

Stone sipped his hot, black sludge and grimaced. "They haven't gotten away with it." He glanced up at the clock on the wall over the entrance door. It was 8:15 "What time did the unit get there?"

Becks looked at his watch. "Eight o'clock, maybe."

"Who is it?"

"Williams."

Stone took another sip. "He make this coffee?"

"No."

"He bring in these muffins?"

"No. Why?"

"I didn't want to have to shoot him when I got over there."

Becks shook his head, spun on his heels, and returned to his office.

Stone placed a lid on his cup, shot a look toward Becks' door to make sure it was closed, and then grabbed a muffin. He was almost to the door when he heard Becks shout, "Enjoy that muffin!"

Sonofabitch.

Stone sat his coffee cup on the dashboard of his black 2012 Ford F-150 and placed the muffin in the seat next to him. When he got to the street the traffic was heavy. *Really,* he thought. *No one's going to let me out of this parking lot?* He scanned the truck for the note Becks had given him, and then remembered it was still stuck to his forehead. He quickly grabbed it and then looked at the passengers in each passing car, hoping none of them had seen.

He waited for another forty-five seconds or so and then flipped on his light bar. The traffic halted, and Stone took a right out of the parking lot onto Route 28, heading south.

*****

Tim Wilson turned the ancient green Buick Le Sabre right off of North Street onto Route 28. Howard Evans was riding shotgun and Jeff Phelps and Eldon Torres were in the back seat. Eldon reached forward and swatted Tim in the back of the head. "Come on, Wilson, you drive like an old lady," he bitched. "For Chrissakes, pass these slowpokes."

"I'm not passing anyone," Wilson answered. "There's a solid yellow line."

As they drove past the police station Howard pointed saying "Yeah, Wilson, pass all these cars with a cop sitting right there."

Torres glanced over at the black F-150 that was waiting for a spot in the traffic to open. "Sorry, I didn't see the cop."

"That's because you're stupid," Wilson observed.

"What the hell's that cop got on his forehead?" Howard asked.

Torres slapped Wilson in the back of the head again. "Shut up. I'm not stupid."

"You slap me one more time, and I'll shoot you and leave you in the woods for the bears."

Phelps laughed.

"What the hell are you laughing at, Phelps? You're only here because your uncle owns the storage units."

"And because it was mine and Howard's idea," Phelps reminded him.

"Genius plan," Torres said. "Rob houses all summer, stick the shit in storage units, then sell it all in the winter. Great plan."

"I didn't hear you come up with anything better."

"If I had of come up with something, it would have been something that would have made us money now and not five months from now. Why can't we sell some of the stuff now?"

"Don't be stupid," Phelps said. "Selling that shit now would *sure* as hell get us caught."

"I'm warning you: Don't call me stupid.'"

"We need gas," Wilson said, and pulled into a Nice N Easy convenience store.

"Need air in that front tire, too," said Howard.

Wilson pulled the Buick up to one of the pumps and shut off the engine. He reached into his pocket, pulled out a fifty dollar bill, and waved it over the back of the front seat. "Tell them I'm getting twenty bucks worth and see if they have a cheap tire pressure gauge."

Torres snatched the fifty. "I got it," he said and climbed out of the car.

Wilson got out of the car too, leaving his door open, and looked back through the opening at Phelps. "Go in with him. I don't want him doing anything stupid."

Torres raised his hand to smack Wilson, and Wilson quickly put his hand under his shirt, grabbing the grip of his 9mm. "Just try it."

"I have a gun too, Wilson," said Torres with a mirthless grin. He turned, and together with Phelps, walked into the convenience store.

Howard climbed out of the passenger seat, shut the door, and leaned his arms on the roof of the car. "We never should have let Torres in on this thing. He's always doing something crazy."

"Like killing two dogs?" Wilson looked back at the pump to see if it had cleared. "Wasn't my idea to let him in." He tried to see inside the store. "What's taking so long?"

*****

Chuck Little, now dressed in his khaki forest ranger uniform, hollered up the stairs, "If you're coming to work with me, Bobby, you better get moving!"

"I'm coming, I'm coming!" the-eight-year old shouted back.

"That kid takes longer to get ready than you do."

Alice ignored the jab. She stood staring into the kitchen sink with one hand on her belly and the other on the counter top.

"What's the matter with you?" Chuck asked knowingly.

"My stomach is a little off this morning," Alice replied.

"Huh, that's weird. I was hoping you were going to make me breakfast this morning."

"Can you and Bobby grab something on the way?"

"Too sick to make breakfast, are ya?"

"I'm not sick. I just have an upset stomach."

"Come on, Bobby!" Chuck yelled, and then turned back to his wife. "A sickness in the morning, I wonder if there's a medical term for that." Chuck looked at the ceiling as if in deep thought and tugged at his long beard. "Sickness. In. The. Morning. Hey, I know: They should call it morning sickness. What might cause such a thing, I wonder?"

"I'm not amused, Chuck. I take it you saw the pregnancy test in the bathroom."

"Yeah, and it looks like someone didn't study for her test … because you failed."

Alice turned and leaned back against the cabinet. "Or maybe I passed with flying colors."

Chuck walked over to his wife and put his arms around her. He bent down and kissed her on top of her head. "You're lucky you're the teacher's pet."

Bobby leapt from the third step, landing in the kitchen. "I'm ready."

"Then lets hit the road, toad," Chuck said, and kissed his wife on the lips. "I love you."

"I love you too."

Bobby ran for the front door.

"Do I get a kiss good bye?" his mother asked.

"Nope," Bobby responded, yanked open the door, and ran for the truck.

"I hope this one's a girl," Alice sighed.

*****

Eric Stone pulled his cell phone from his pocket and dialed.

"Hello?"

"Williams?"

"Yeah."

"It's Stone. You still on Riverside Drive?"

"Roger that."

"Where are the homeowners?"

"They're next door at some friend's house. They were pretty shaken up."

"I bet. Wait there for me. I'm stopping for gas, then I'll be right over. And Williams, don't touch anything."

"Roger that," Williams said and hung up.

Stone tossed his cell into the passenger seat. "Roger that," he grumbled as he pulled into the Nice N Easy parking lot and up to one of the pumps. He reached over, grabbed the blueberry muffin, and unwrapped it. He took a bite and sat it on the dashboard next to his coffee. He took a sip of the coffee. "Yuck."

He shut off his engine, got out, and poured the coffee out onto the black top. He glanced over to the other side of the pumps at the two young men standing next to a green Buick. "Some people just don't know how to make coffee," he commented.

Wilson looked over the top of the car at Howard and then back at Stone. He smiled nervously and said, "Yeah."

Stone waved to Chuck Little when he saw him pull into the parking lot and park in a spot in front of the store.

Then he pulled his debit card out of his money clip. He placed it in the slot and quickly pulled it out. The pump cleared and Stone began pumping his gas. "You boys up here on vacation?"

Wilson nodded his head. "Yeah."

"Where ya stayin'" Stone asked, as his eyes went from one of the Buick's side windows to the other.

"The hotel," Wilson answered.

Stone chuckled. "There's a *few* hotels."

"Are we doing something wrong?" Howard asked.

"Not that I know of. Why do you ask?" Stone replied.

"It seems like you're busting our balls or something."

"Just being friendly."

Howard opened his door and got back in the car.

Wilson stretched his neck, trying to see inside the store. "What are they doing in there?" he whispered to himself.

Stone replaced the gas nozzle and decided to go in for a cup of coffee, and to say hi to his friend Chuck.

*****

"You want a slice of this breakfast pizza or do you want one of those egg and cheese sandwiches?" Chuck Little asked his son.

"I just want chips and a soda," Bobby answered.

"You're not having chips and soda for breakfast."

"Fine. What's on the pizza?"

"It's breakfast pizza," Chuck answered as he got in line behind two young men. "It has egg, bacon, and cheese on it."

"Eggs ... on pizza? That's gross."

"There's no yolk; it's *scrambled* eggs." Chuck noticed an air pressure gauge sticking out of one of the guy's back pockets. In the same guy's hand was a fifty-dollar bill. The other twenty-something was holding a twelve-ounce Pepsi.

"He has a soda," Bobby pointed out.

"He's older than you," Chuck answered.

"Not *much* older."

Torres turned around and looked up at Chuck, all six-foot-six of him, and then down at Bobby. "What's the matter, kid, your old man won't buy you a soda?"

"No, he's being unfair" Bobby answered.

"Bobby," Chuck scolded.

Torres turned back around. "My old man was a prick too."

Bobby tugged on his father's shirt. "Dad, did you hear what he said?"

"I heard, son. Never mind them."

Phelps jabbed Torres in the ribs. "Knock it off."

"I'm just sayin', the kid wants a soda, Ranger Rick should buy him a fuckin' soda."

Phelps said, "Watch the language, man." He turned and looked up at Chuck. "You'll have to excuse my friend," he said. "He's had a hard life."

"I figured he must have," Chuck said.

A woman two customers ahead of Phelps and Torres was counting change out of a small coin purse.

"Come on, lady, we ain't got all friggin' day," Torres said.

"Why don't you calm down, pal," Chuck said.

Torres spun around. "Why don't you shut the fuck up, *pal*? Or maybe I'll shut you up. You think you look tough in that uniform, huh. Yogi-Bear-lovin' dick."

Bobby impulsively covered his mouth with his little hand. Chuck kept his cool.

Phelps grabbed Torres by the arm and pulled him back around. "Knock it off. You're gonna get us in trouble. He turned and gave Chuck an apologetic shrug.

Phelps and Torres were up, and Phelps sat his drink on the counter.

"Finally," said Torres. He slapped the fifty down next to the register. He turned and pointed toward the pumps. "We're getting twenty in gas, *and* the soda."

Chuck reached down and pulled the pressure gauge from Torres' pocket and tossed it on the counter. "You forgot the tire pressure gauge," he said.

Torres reached under the front of his shirt and yanked the .38 from his waistband. "I warned you, Ranger Rick!" he shouted.

"No!" Phelps screamed.

Torres brought his arm around and Chuck grabbed his wrist. Torres fired once into the ceiling and once through the front window, shattering the glass.

Chuck forced Torres' arm downward as he brought up his knee. The gun flew from Torres' grip and hit the floor, sliding across the room.

Two shots sounded outside, and a second later two more.

Phelps went for the gun and dove on it. As he rolled over, Chuck was running toward him.

Phelps aimed the gun and screamed, "Stop!"

They heard another gunshot from outside.

Chuck froze. He reached out and took hold of his son's shirt and pulled the boy behind him.

"Stop," Phelps repeated. "Just … nobody move."

*****

Stone flinched and instinctively went for his gun at the sound of the breaking glass. Wilson went for his gun as well. Stone jumped behind the gas pump. Wilson fired twice, once hitting the pump and once hitting Stones windshield.

Stone crouched down, came out from behind the pump, and fired two shots through the open passenger side window. Both bullets whizzed past Howard's face and struck Wilson in the abdomen.

Howard dropped to his side and crawled across the car seat after Wilson's gun.

"Don't do it!" Stone shouted.

Howard, half in and half out of the vehicle, grabbed the weapon, and Stone put one through the back of his skull.

*****

"Everyone away from the entrance!" Torres yelled. He walked over to Phelps. "Give me the gun, Phelps"

Phelps obeyed and then ran to the front door. "There's a cop out there," he said.

"Shit!" Torres smacked himself in the head twice with the hand holding the .38. "Shit, shit, shit. What are we gonna do?"

"Just lay the gun down," Chuck said.

"Shut up!" Torres shouted. He pointed the gun at Chuck and then at the kid behind the counter. "Come out from behind there. Get over there." He pointed to the far corner of the store.

The cashier, in his early twenties, whose name-tag read DAMIEN, slowly came out from behind the register. His hands in the air, he walked in the direction Torres was pointing the gun.

Chuck, his son, and the other ten customers were still frozen in place.

Torres waved the .38 around the room. "Everyone follow him, and sit down on the floor," he ordered. He pointed the gun at Damien. "Is there any other workers here?"

"Yes," Damien answered.

Torres' eyes darted around the store. "Where?"

"He took out the garbage."

"Phelps!" Torres shouted. "Get away from the door. Go find the other employee."

The customers slowly made their way to the corner of the store, and began taking a seat on the floor.

Phelps ran down the aisle between the soda and beer coolers to a rear exit. He pushed open the door and looked around. Seeing no one, he pulled the door closed, and returned to the store. "There isn't anybody out there," he told Torres. "He must have ran when he heard the shots."

"What's back there?" Torres asked.

"Trees and then the river … I think. Should we make a run for it?"

Sirens sounded in the distance.

"Yeah, let's go."

Torres and Phelps ran for the door. Torres shoved it open.

"Move!" Chuck shouted, grabbing one of the female customers by the arm. "Run for the door."

"Come on, come on," Damien said, helping an elderly woman to her feet.

Everyone ran.

Torres took two steps out the rear door and a patrol car, lights flashing and sirens wailing, skidded to a stop a few feet in front of them. Torres fired two shots into the windshield. "Go back, go back!" He and Phelps turned and went back inside, closing the door behind them.

Torres quickly ran back down the aisle. "Stop!" he shouted, pointing his weapon at Chuck and Damien, the only two who hadn't made it out of the store.

Chuck and Damien froze.

"Get back over there," Torres ordered, pointing his gun. "Back over in the corner and get on the ground. What's going on out there?"

"There's two more cop cars out front," Phelps said "and an ambulance."

Chuck sat with his back against the soda fountain. "You only have two shots left, ya know."

Torres trained his gun on Chuck. "One for each of you."

"If you don't waste any more."

"Maybe I should just kill you both right now."

Damien remained silent.

"That would be stupid," Chuck said. "You haven't hurt anyone yet. You could put down that gun and walk out that door."

"And go right to prison."

"Would you rather go for a couple years, or the rest of your life?"

"Shut up, just shut up!"

Phelps made his way to the back of the store. "What are we gonna do, Eldon?"

"Just stay calm, Phelps. Let me think," Torres replied.

*****

Gun drawn and pointing downward at his side, Eric Stone ran toward the fleeing customers. "Get behind the cars!" he shouted. His eyes quickly scanned the faces in the crowd, trying to determine if any of them were the suspects. He spotted Bobby Little. "Bobby, over here."

Bobby ran to Stone and threw his arms around the investigator. "My dad is still in there," he said.

"I know," Stone replied, picking up the eight-year-old and running for cover.

Two more units pulled into the parking lot, and a few seconds later an ambulance was on the scene.

Chief Becks arrived in an unmarked unit, swung open his door and, crouching ran to Stone. "What the hell is going on?"

Stone looked down at the young boy beside him. "Bobby, how many of them are in there?"

"Two," Bobby answered. "One guy has a gun."

Becks turned toward one of the other officers. "Get this road blocked off, and round up everybody who was in that store and keep them together." He turned to the EMTs. "Get these two bodies out of here."

Bobby looked behind him at the dead body of Howard Evans and cringed. Stone turned him back around and sat him down behind his rear truck tire.

"Don't move, little buddy," Stone said.

Bobby pulled his knees up to his chest and wrapped his arms around his legs.

"Have you established contact, Stone?" Becks asked.

"I was just about to when they all came running out." Stone opened his driver's side door and grabbed his cell phone from the passenger seat. He went through his contacts until he came to Chuck Little, and hit the call icon.

*****

Chuck felt his phone vibrate in his shirt pocket the second his ringtone began playing "Brickhouse."

Torres spun around, his .38 pointing at Chuck. "What the hell is that?"

"'Brickhouse by the Commodores," Chuck responded. "You want me to answer it?"

"Answer it."

Chuck pulled out the cell. "Nice N Easy Grocery Shoppes, we do things right for you. Chuck speaking. How can I help you?"

"I think you missed your calling, Chuck," said Stone.

"Hi, Eric. How's your day going?"

"Good. Yours?"

"Chucky Jr. puked all over the floor, my wife is pregnant again, and now this."

"Oh, congratulations. Hey, can I speak to whoever thinks they're in charge in there?"

"Sure." Chuck held the phone out to Torres. "It's for you."

Torres grabbed the phone. "Hello."

"Good morning," Stone said. "This is Investigator Eric Stone with the Town of Webb Police Department. And who am I speaking with?"

"None of your business, that's who."

Phelps was hiding behind the newspaper rack as he gazed out the window at the commotion they had caused.

"Okay, then what should I call you?" Stone asked.

"You can call me the man who's gonna kill these two guys in here if you don't let us leave."

"So, you need a vehicle. Is there anything else I can get you?"

Becks was on his cell phone with the State Police. When he hung up he whispered to Stone, "The staties are sending a negotiator. He should be here in a half hour or so."

Stone placed his hand over the cell's mic. "We might not have that long."

"Where's my friends?" Torres asked.

"Your friends are in custody," said Stone.

"I want you to let them go," Torres instructed. "Have them drive the car up to the door and we'll get in. We'll take one of these guys with us. When we're sure no one's following us we'll let him go."

"Give us some time to clear the road. There's a lot of traffic backed up out here," Stone said.

"You have ten minutes. If that car isn't pulling up out front in ten minutes, I put a bullet in these guys' heads." Torres hung up and tossed the phone back to Chuck.

Phelps duck-walked towards Torres. "They're not gonna just let us go," he said.

"Everything's going to be fine," Torres said. "The four of us will head for Canada."

"Head for Canada? What then?"

"Then we're home free. They don't have jurisdiction in Canada."

Phelps put his hands on top of his head. "What are you, stupid? They don't need jurisdiction. The goddamn Mounties will just arrest us and send us back as soon we cross the border."

"Stop calling me stupid!" Torres shouted. "I'm not stupid."

"Not stupid? This is all your fault. All you had to do was keep your stupid mouth shut and pay for the goddamn tire gauge." Phelps started toward the door with his hands in the air. "I'm done. I'm giving myself up."

"Stop!" Torres hollered.

Phelps kept walking. He was almost to the door.

"I said *stop!*" Torres raised his weapon and aimed. "Please." He fired once into Phelps' back.

Phelps fell forward, hitting the floor. His blood seeped out from beneath him.

Torres ran to his friend and knelt down beside him. "Why didn't you stop?"

Chuck leapt to his feet and ran toward Torres.

Torres heard him coming and quickly stood. He spun around and fired his last round, hitting Chuck in the shoulder. The bullet felt like a bee sting to the towering forest ranger and the adrenaline pumping through his veins.

Chuck gave vent to a primal scream and smashed into Torres at full speed, and together they flew through the glass doors onto the sidewalk.

Becks and Stone ran across the parking lot, their guns pointing at the two men lying on the concrete. As they reached them, Chuck Little rolled off of Torres' lifeless body. A shard of glass had pierced his neck, killing him instantly.

"Lay still," Stone said to his friend. "You, ah—" He pointed at the glass sticking out of Chuck's arm, and then at the one protruding from his thigh.

"Ouch," Chuck said, and let his head fall back on the concrete. "Ouch."

One Last Round

I do some of my best thinking in the bathroom—not on the toilet, but in the shower. After I've soaped up, rinsed off, and washed my hair, I just like to stand there with the warm water running over my shoulders and down my back. Winter is the best, when the warmest place is in the shower, but spring is good too.

I think about a lot of things in those seven or eight minutes. I wonder whether or not I was a good enough father. Did I spend enough time with them? Did I do enough with them, and for them? I don't think I did, but all three of my children seem to like me; they laugh at my bad jokes, they tell me they love me, and they give me hugs every time they see me. They've all moved out now. The house is so quiet these days, compared to what it was ten years ago. I think about the noises that used to annoy me, and how much I wish I could hear them now. No one interrupts my television viewing, no one loses the remote control, and no one fights over toys in the background.

I wonder if I was a good enough husband. I did my best, I think. I was probably better than some, and worse than others. I should have saved more money. There's fights I regret having. We had problems, just like everyone else, but I'm glad she's still here.

For some reason I spend a lot of time wondering if anyone would miss me if I were gone. My parents and siblings seem to enjoy being around me, but something in my head tells me they would be better off without me. I don't know why.

I've often thought about suicide. I've even secretly wished there was some way to die—just to see if anyone cried—and then come back to life. Some days I feel like I want to die. I know I would never kill myself, mostly because I'm a coward. I've heard people say that suicide is the easy way out … the coward's way out, but I think it takes an awfully brave person to take that step.

A week ago I had my yearly physical. The nurse weighed me and then brought me into one of the examining rooms. "Can you pull up that shirtsleeve?" she asked.

After taking my blood pressure, and then my temperature, she sat down at a round stool with wheels in front of a desktop computer. "In the last few weeks have you felt hopeless or had any thoughts of suicide?"

My answer was, of course going to be no, but before I forced the words out, she gave me a crooked smile and said, "I know, right? We have to ask now—new health laws and all."

I smiled back and nodded my head in agreement at how crazy those questions were, but at the same time I thought, *What if I was about to reveal my biggest secret? What if my answer was going to be yes? What if I was about to beg for the help I knew I probably needed?* Oh well.

I think about work. I think about money. I think about the water bill.

"You okay in there?" my wife calls out.

I reach down and turn off the water, slide back the shower curtain, and grab the towel I had laid on the ceramic sink top.

Do I suffer from depression? How would I know? Is there a checklist like the ones for alcoholics? I know I don't score very well on those ones. I probably drink too much. I'm never drunk, I go to work every day. Maybe I drink just enough to keep from putting a gun in my mouth. Yeah, let's go with that. We'll call it *justifiable semi-alcoholic tendencies*. There—I made up a new disease.

I unzip one of the pockets in my golf bag and check to make sure I have plenty of tees and balls. I can golf all day with the same tee, but I've been known to lose three balls in nine holes. I'm not the greatest golfer in the world, I might even be the worst, but I enjoy it just the same. I don't use a cart; I prefer walking. Driving around in those carts just isn't as relaxing.

I bought a new driver this winter and I can't wait to see how that works out. I would imagine that the old driver was the one thing that kept me off the tour.

I pick up my bag, throw the strap over my shoulder, and head down the driveway. I set the bag next to the trunk of my car and head back inside. My bag, clubs, and shoes have a combined value of about fifty bucks, so it's fine to leave them in the driveway while I go back in for the keys.

"I'm heading out," I say.

"Did you find anyone to go with you?" my wife asks.

"No."

"Won't that be boring?"

I grin. "Not hardly. There's a big difference between quiet, and boring."

She walks toward me with a stack of folded laundry in her hand, and pauses to kiss me good bye. "Have fun."

"You too. I love you."

"I love you too," she says, and heads up the stairs.

I check my cell phone again, just to make sure no one has changed their mind and decided to join me. No missed calls.

I walk out the door and gaze at the sky; not one cloud, and the temperature has risen to about sixty-five degrees. What a beautiful day. I hope the course isn't crowded. I check my watch. 7:25. I pop the trunk and load the clubs.

"Beautiful day," says the woman behind the counter.

"Sure is," I agree.

"They were calling for rain."

"They never seem to know what they're talking about."

She slides a score card in front of me. "Eighteen?"

"Nine … and no cart."

She grabs a golf pencil and sets it on top of the score card. "Twelve bucks."

I turn and walk toward the cooler. "I'm gonna grab a soda too."

"Thirteen bucks."

I set the soda on the counter and take out a twenty. "Here ya go."

She counts out my change and hands it back to me. "Good luck."

"Thanks," I say, and head out through the door toward the sprawling acres of green.

About halfway between the clubhouse and the first tee I pause and remove my cardigan. *Could you ask for a better day?* I think. I unzip the largest pouch in the bag, stuff my sweater inside, and continue my journey. I glance back at the parking lot as I walk along; my car is still the only one in the lot.

I tee up my ball, remove my new driver from the bag and take a few practice swings. The first hole is a par four, but a halfway decent golfer can be on the green in one.

Head down. Knees slightly bent. Don't take your eyes off the ball. I swing.

I know it's perfect the minute I hit it; there's no mistaking that sound. I watch as the ball slowly climbs and then descends. It hits the ground and rolls about twenty yards. I'm about six feet from the edge of the green. Nice!

I look over at the parking lot and see four old guys climbing out of a gray Toyota Corolla. They'll never catch up to me.

When I reach my ball I pull my chipper from the bag. I've always had good luck with this club. I bought it at a used sporting goods store years ago; "Mr. Chipper," it says on the head. I often wondered if there was a Mrs. Chipper, or if Mr. Chipper just played the field, hopping from one club to the next.

On the seventh hole, the one that heads back toward the road, I tee up my ball, the same ball I started the game with. On my third practice swing, something at the edge of the tree line catches my eye. I drop the head of my driver to the grass and examine the area. It's a small child, a pale-skinned little girl.

I put up my hand. "Hi," I say, but she doesn't answer. I shrug my shoulders, pick up my club, and swing. I watch the ball sail over a small hill out of sight. Not being able to see the flag from where I am, I hope that it went in the right direction.

I return my club to the bag and grab the handle of my handcart. The little girl is still watching. I look behind her to see if she is accompanied by anyone.

"Are you by yourself?" I ask.

She pushes her long, thin, blond hair away from her face, but says nothing.

Searching for anyone, I only see the four old men just finishing up at the fifth hole. "Where's your mom and dad?" I probe. She still doesn't say anything, so I take one last look around, leave my cart, and walk toward her. "What's your name?" I ask.

The girl throws her arms around me and says, "Daddy!"

Oh boy. I look around again, this time with a slight feeling of embarrassment. "I'm not your daddy, kid." I don't notice any house behind the row of trees; the only houses nearby are across the road, beyond the seventh hole.

"Daddy," she repeats.

"Nope," I insist, prying her arms from around my legs. "Are you out here all by yourself?" I check my watch. 9:07. I crouch down and take her tiny little hands in mine. "Can you say anything other than daddy?"

A big smile instantly appears across her flat little face, and her almond-shaped eyes squint even more. "Yes," she answers.

"Yes *and* daddy. Do you golf?"

She shakes her head no, the smile still on her face.

I return to my handcart and she follows me. With my left hand I grab the handle of my cart and with my right I reach out to her. She takes my hand and together we walk toward the seventh hole.

When we reach the top of the hill, I see my ball; it's about fifty yards from the green. "Not too shabby," I comment, and we continue on.

I let go of my cart and the little girl's hand at the same time. "What do you think?" I ask. "Nine iron, or maybe a pitching wedge." I choose the nine iron. "Step back." I decide not to take a practice swing and then smack the top of the ball, sending it rolling forward about three feet. "Goddammit!"

"Goddammit!" she repeats.

"Great. Daddy, yes, and now Goddammit."

I see her little mouth starting to form the word again. "No," I warn her sternly. "That's not a very nice word." She quickly closes her mouth.

I take hold of my golf towel and wipe the dirt from the club head. I swing again and this time the ball drops onto the green and rolls into the hole. "Yes!" I shout.

"Yes!" she repeats.

I reward her with a smile, take her hand, and we head toward the green. I let go of my bag and her hand. "Don't go near the road," I say. "Can you grab my ball?"

She runs across the green and reaches into the hole, grabs the ball, yanks it out, and shows it to me.

I pull my scorecard from my pocket and stare at it for a second. When she gets back to me, she hands me the ball and I say, "Ya know, even if I bogie these next two holes, I'll still get my best score ever." I return the card to my pocket and notice a woman across the road. It looks like she is searching for something, and I think I know what it is.

I pick up the girl and start across the road. "Hey!" I shout.

The woman looks over and instantly there's a look of relief. "Oh thank God!" she shouts, and runs toward us.

I hand the woman her daughter and point toward the seventh tee. "I found her up there."

She hugs her daughter as hard as she can. "Thank you, thank you."

I walk with them to the other side of the street. "She kept calling me daddy."

The woman laughs. "She calls every man daddy."

"I figured."

The woman thanks me a few more times and even hugs me. As they walk up their front steps I start back across the road. When I reach the solid yellow line, I hear her call out, "Thanks again."

I turn and wave.

Just as I take a step, I hear a horn and the squeal of tires. Everything flashes white and then goes dark. When I open my eyes, I'm staring up at the cloudless sky. I feel like I'm lying in a puddle—wet. I reach up to wipe the water from my face, but the water is red and thick.

An old man leans over me. "Lay still," he urges. He sounds so far away.

I try to speak but am choking on something. There's a taste of copper in my mouth, like after a nosebleed.

I don't want to die.

COMING SUMMER 2016

Most Likely to Die

From the Tales of Dan Coast

COMING FALL 2016

Jake Stellar

The Obedience of Fools

We Call it Suicide

A Dunquin Cove Story

ALSO BY RODNEY RIESEL

Sleeping Dogs Lie
From the Tales of Dan Coast

A mystery set in the Florida Keys follows Dan Coast, an unlicensed private detective of sorts, as he is hired to find the missing boyfriend of a woman who herself soon ends up missing. When someone from the woman's past unexpectedly shows up at Dan's home, with a story of faked deaths and missing life insurance money; Dan along with his sidekick Red set out to find the money, and the woman.

ISBN: 978-0-9883503-0-4

Ocean Floors
From the Tales of Dan Coast

The second installment in the Dan Coast series, Ocean Floors, is a tale of mystery and possible romance when a chance meeting with a beautiful young woman leads Dan and his trusted sidekick Red down a road of murder and kidnapping. Join Dan and Red as they try to solve the murder while searching for a missing friend.

ISBN: 978-0-9894877-0-2

North Murder Beach
A Jake Stellar Novel

The first installment of the story of North Myrtle Beach police detective, Jake Stellar. The spring bike rallies have ended, the spring breakers have all gone back to school, and the summer tourist season is a few weeks away. What better time for a police officer to take a nice quiet relaxing week off from work? That's what Jake Stellar had in mind. That is until someone from his past resurfaces to remind him of a terrible secret he has spent years trying to forget. In North Murder Beach, a story of revenge, Jake is unwillingly and violently forced to confront his secret from his past.

ISBN: 978-0-9894877-1-9

The Coast of Christmas Past
From the Tales of Dan Coast

Coast of Christmas Past is the third book in the Dan Coast series of books. Dan Coast is all set to spend Christmas just the same way he has every year for the past few years; alone and drunk. But when uninvited, unexpected guests arrive and throw a wrench into his holiday plans he is forced to sober up (slightly), and throw on a smile. Just when it seems nothing else could go wrong, a close friend is injured in what appears, to the police, to be a drug deal gone bad. Dan Coast and his sidekick, Red jump into action to find the truth while their friend lies unconscious in the hospital.

ISBN: 978-0-9894877-3-3

The Man in Room Number Four
The Dunquin Cove Series

When a mysterious stranger arrives in the small coastal town of Dunquin Cove, Maine it appears as though Claire and her young son, Mica's prayers have been answer.

But who is he, and why is he really here? Join Claire and her guests at the Colsome House Bed and Breakfast as they piece together the mystery of the Man in Room Number Four.

ISBN: 978-0-9894877-2-6

Ship of Fools
From the Tales of Dan Coast

Ship of Fools is the fourth book in The Tales of Dan Coast series and begins where Coasts of Christmas Past left off. Find out how Dan deals with the death of a young friend, while looking into the disappearance of a new friend's sister. Join Dan, Red, and Skip as they fumble their way through a new mystery.

ISBN: 978-0-9894877-4-0

Beach Shoot
A Jake Stellar Series

It's a beautiful Sunday morning in North Myrtle Beach and Emily Bowen, a wife and mother of four, lies dying on the beach. Jake Stellar returns in Beach Shoot, a new mystery by Rodney Riesel.

Beach Shoot is the second Jake Stellar book and sequel to the Amazon Best Seller North Murder Beach. In Beach Shoot, Jake finds himself teamed up with the most unlikely of partners, his nemesis and fellow detective Avis Lint. Join Jake and Avis as they piece together the clues in this thrilling new mystery.

ISBN: 978-0-9894877-5-7

Return to Dunquin Cove
The Dunquin Cove Series

It's been almost six months since the day ex-hitman, Ben Dunning turned up in Dunquin Cove, Maine, not knowing where or who he was. He's lived a quiet, peaceful life in the small town, but now his old life is calling him back. As Ben plans a trip to Boston in search of his past, little does he know that trouble is brewing in Dunquin Cove. Two strangers have arrived with the promise of safety and security. Join Ben and the people of Dunquin Cove as they band together to prove they can take care of themselves and their town.

ISBN: 978-0-9894877-7-1

Double Trouble

From the Tales of Dan Coast

Shortly after Walter and Warren Bowman arrive in Key West in search of a sister they never knew they had, Warren disappears. With nowhere else to turn, Walter enlists the help of Dan Coast. Join Dan as he and sidekick Red Baxter search for the missing Bowman family members, while dealing with the fallout of an ongoing case.

ISBN: 978-0-9894877-9-5

When Death Returns

A Jake Stellar Series

Has a serial killer from the past returned to North Myrtle Beach? Jake Stellar is back in When Death Returns. Join Jake and his partner Avis Lint in this exciting third installment of the Jake Stellar series as they investigate a homicide that eerily echoes the past.

ISBN: 978-0-9971149-0-4